Far East Crossfire

"*Dueling with the Devil*"

Stephen L. Thompson

Far East Crossfire

Books by Stephen L. Thompson

The Crossfire Series

Colorado Crossfire
International Crossfire
Israeli Crossfire
Believer's Crossfire
Spirit Crossfire
Faith Crossfire
Chinese Crossfire
Texas Crossfire
Dark Crossfire
Island Crossfire
Jagged Crossfire
Violent Crossfire
Russian Crossfire
Nuclear Crossfire
End Times Crossfire
Revelation Crossfire
Gates of Hell Crossfire
Assassin's Crossfire
Global Crossfire
Far East Crossfire

The SFO Series

Station Force One – Onset

Far East Crossfire

Beginning their last three years on Earth, the Crossfire Team has already managed to thoroughly irritate two of the remaining world powers, China and Russia. China wants the secret to the team's new Base of Operations, which is their new ship, the "Sword."The Sword started life as an advanced naval project for a fully supported battalion of Marines with three nuclear reactors and loaded with leading-edge technology.

Russia wants revenge against the Team because that unique 777-foot-long military ship destroyed all five of Russia's latest half-billion dollar submarines per God's command, after they attacked the Sword. Like Satan and the Anti-Christ's New World Government, which includes America, Russia now seeks total destruction of the Team. The Sword is protected by a "Force Generator field" that prevents any force from damaging it.

- Stephen L. Thompson

Far East Crossfire

Published by
Stephen L. Thompson
Facebook.com/CrossfireNovelSeries

ISBN- 978-1-943879-29-8

Published in the United States of America

Foreword

To my Christian readers –
The Crossfire series of action/adventure stories include depictions of violence, which are unusual in Christian literature. It would be nice if there were no conflict or violence in our world. But we live in a time when evil is increasing instead of diminishing, when some men seem to be controlled by selfishness, madness, or evil forces. When the enemies of decent mankind are bent on subjugation of other men and women, righteous men and women must stand against evil. The yoke of oppression is not lifted by prayer alone. God is our shepherd and we are his sheep. As long as there are wolves about, God will use some of us as sheep dogs to defend the rest of us. These stories are about people like that and the forces they fight against. The stories describe violence because it occurs in the real world and it is active in the lives of all people whether they recognize it or not.

To my non-Christian readers –
The Crossfire series include depictions of spiritual warfare and spiritual activity with which the non-Christian may not be familiar. These stories describe the realms and activities of both God and Satan because they are real and active in the lives of all people whether they recognize it or not.

Steve Thompson

CHAPTER ONE

The pre-combat silence was electric with anticipation. Mark Connelly reviewed his preparations to ensure the team was as prepared as they could be for the coming battle. This situation was really different than their usual battles lately. Because they were battling humans instead of demons, and the number of the enemy forces was not overwhelming, the team members did not have the use of their Force Generator fields, which prevented any damage to their persons. Also, since these were not demonic enemies, their armor and swords would not be involved either. That meant that they were back to square one. They did have improved body armor and heavier weapons. But it would take God to give them the victory.

Their attackers this time were definitely the best that Russia could field, Spetznas Special Forces. In the last decade, they had upgraded their weapons and tactics to the same level as the American Special Forces such as the Delta Teams. Mark knew the troops involved in this attack were seasoned troops and very professional. After seeking God for the best way to overcome their adversaries he had incorporated his best ideas and the most exceptional combat strategies he could. But he still did not have his normal confidence prior to the battle. Something was off about this battle and he just could not put his mental finger on the oddness. In an attempt to put things in order, he thought back to how they ended up here against this group of combat specialists.

-----------------------******-----------------------

Three days ago, he had been enjoying a day off from training the newer members in advanced combat techniques. He had spent a good afternoon and evening with his wife Sarah sharing some time and affection. Today they had a casual morning together and then word came to them that a group of Jewish families were being harassed in Antalya, Turkey by some soldiers and there were reports

1

of "evil spirits", or demons, along with the soldiers terrorizing the people.

The "Sword" was not too far from the area and Jack had them sail to the area to check out the situation. Sarah and two of the female Jewish sailors made their way into the town acting as locals. With their darker skin and black hair, they blended into the population. They went into the marketplace and casually talked about nothing much with some of the knowledgeable citizens. Before long, they broached the subject of hearing about some soldiers treating some of the Jews poorly. Two of the local women knew about the "filthy" Russian troops and the area they were in.

After changing subjects and discussing possible work available, they wandered away and slowly approached the buildings identified by the locals. Sarah and the two women passed a building and saw several soldiers in the front of the building. One of the soldiers called to them in the local version of Turkish. Sarah was familiar with the language and led the man on but she did not stop walking away from the building.

The man grabbed a hat and hurried after the women. Sarah turned down a dirty alley as the man caught up and flirted with her. One of the other women acted out a bit of jealousy about the man who was eyeing both Sarah and her when the third woman carefully slid a hypodermic syringe into the side of the man's neck. He did not feel the needle but suddenly got groggy and collapsed to the ground.

Sarah looked at the woman she had believed was simply a sailor. "You are very good at this business. Why is that?"

Chana smiled conspiringly at Sarah and said in Hebrew, "We've used this dance many times in the past when we needed sailors in foreign ports."

Sarah smiled back, "I see, is this just a knock-out drug or is it also a truth serum?"

Chana tilted her head in question, "It is a crude truth drug. After all, we didn't want really bad men on our boats."

Sarah nodded and pulled out a kit of her own, twenty minutes later they took the man's money and watch to make it look like a robbery and left him in the alley. They made their way back to where Jack and Mark were waiting at a dock and the rubber boat. Fifteen minutes later, they were back on the Sword. Sara thanked Chana and her friend and let them go back to their duties. She sat down in the War Room and discussed her findings with the men and Laura. "I have to give it to the Russians. They had a good idea how we would scope them out. The man we lured away from their operating base was a prepared plant. He did not have much info other than the size of their force, which was fifty men, Spetznas of course. But he had a prepared message for us."

Mark frowned, "By "us" you mean ...?"

Sarah shook her head, "The Crossfire Team, of course." She sighed, "The message was, "Our country will destroy your team. Today, tomorrow, next week, next year, whatever it takes. You will pay for your killing all our men in the submarines when their weapons could not hurt you. You can meet us tomorrow at our warehouse in Antalya and we will see how good fighters you are in one-on-one combat or we will track your ship wherever you go and attack you whenever you leave your charmed vessel. The choice is yours."

Jack said, "Let's pray and see if God wants us to ignore this challenge or accept it." The two men and two women sought the Lord and inquired as to Heaven's directions. After thirty minutes with no answer, Jack thanked the Lord for His patience and ended the prayer. "What do we do? "

Mark had thought the situation through. "I think we respond to show Russia that the team isn't intimidated by their threats. Also it would keep at least this team from hunting us and interfering with future actions."

Laura suggested, "Let's ignore them and avoid them for a while because they might give up after a while of being unproductive in their chase."

Jack laughed, "Little chance of that. These are not the deciders; they are soldiers under orders. I would guess that those orders don't include giving up."

As Laura and Mark talked, Jack began to pray again. He thanked the Lord for His protection for himself, his wife, and all of the members of the Crossfire Team. He was beginning to worship when The Father spoke to him. "*My son, go up against the Russian soldiers. I will give them into your hand. I have sent My Word to their ruler to not attack your team. Today he rejected Me completely. I will show him that I am God and that I will not mocked! I will use your team to defeat him and his country.*"

Jack thought, "Father, Yahshua said that we have not been anointed to operate against a country. I know you do not make mistakes so please resolve this conflict for me."

"*There is no conflict between My Son's instructions and mine. It is true that you are not going to compete against Russia on their level. The conflict is between Myself and Russia with your team as my weapon. And I will be with you.*"

"Thank you Father. We are blessed by your words and commandments and seek to do your Will in all things in Yahshua's name."

CHAPTER TWO

Jack told the Connellys and Laura what God had told him. Mark was quite clear on the concept of battling Russia troops. But was still not clear about their operating on the "Russia versus the Crossfire Team" level.

Jack grinned. "Just think of us as soldiers for the good side and working for God. We are only the soldiers, not the General who's calling the shots. It's God vs. Russia"

Mark grinned back, "Okay. I've been a soldier before."

----------------------******------------------------

As the past caught up with the present, Mark suddenly identified the oddness he had been feeling. "So ... this is really just a normal Russian Special Forces plan to kill us."

Knowing what he did about Spetznas tactics, Mark urgently sought God in prayer. "Father Yahveh, the Russians are a perverse group of people. In these types of attacks, they minimize their numbers and then overwhelm their opponents through unexpected introduction of massive overkill. Our small numbers will need the use of the force generators to survive this conflict. I pray Father that you will grant us the use of your generators to balance out these tactics in Yahshua's name. Amen"

Mark clearly heard, *"And it is so granted. Destroy these forces to the last man."*

As the sound of bullets striking concrete echoed, Mark hit his "all-call" button, "All Troops, switch on your Force Generators now!" He switched his on and was gratified to see the tiny green LED light up as two ricochets struck his field and fell to the ground.

Mark called the troops again, "Change of plan, all troops move out and take the battle to the enemy, no quarter given, God says to destroy the enemy to the last person. Leave no survivors. Mark moved to the left side of the advancing line of Crossfire warriors. Dozens of enemy rounds struck his field with no effect on him. As his position uncovered enemy soldiers Mark fired for effect and put down all he could hit and then moved on.

All at once, two of the Spetznas on a mobile gun platform with four, heavy machine guns opened up. These gun platforms were normally used as the ZPU series of anti-aircraft guns. Its size and power also made it a useful light anti-armor weapon on the BTR series of vehicles. It could unleash a lethal stream of heavy bullets to strafe ground troops but it proved useless against God's power in the Force Generators. One of the SOG troops used a Light Anti-Tank Weapon or LAW to launch a missile, which blew the entire ZPU vehicle to pieces.

New, even heavier rounds came slamming into the area of the team members from above. Mark instantly recognized the three attack helicopters as being Mil Mi-28 "Havocs" which were Russian, all-weather, day-night, tandem two-seat, anti-armor attack helicopters. Heavily armored and armed they could be a fearsome opponent in normal combat. Three of the SOG warriors took stances with the latest version of the American/Israeli-made "Stinger" anti-aircraft shoulder-fired missiles. This tactic would not work normally because the Havoc would destroy the missile launcher by flying directly at it and use its heavy nose cannon to saturate the launch site before the missile could be launched. With the Force Generators protecting the man and the missile launcher, the warriors waited until the helicopters were too close to avoid the missiles and then fired. All three helicopters exploded and the wreckage fell to the ground with tremendous crashes less than a hundred feet away.

Several very heavy explosive shells fell on their battle site. Mark turned and spotted two Russian war ships of the heavy destroyer type using their deck guns to pummel the area while four landing craft brought another hundred soldiers or so to the beach just north of the town.

Mark called the Sword and advised them of the ships and landing craft. The barrage stopped as the troops stormed onto the beach. Sarah ran up to him, "I Thank God for the Force Generators. Otherwise, none of us would have had a chance of surviving this onslaught."

Mark was about to answer when the Sword slammed into the first destroyer, splitting it in half at the amidships.

The sound was hellaciously loud even at that distance. The two halves of the Russian destroyer immediately sank in the shallow water off shore. The Sword immediately drove toward the second ship and repeated the slam-bang operation with an equivalent racket and devastating effect. The Russian sailors on the landing craft wisely abandoned their craft on the beach and sought cover in the town. Four small missiles from the Sword destroyed the landing craft in four more major explosions.

Mark called the Crossfire Team into a new alignment to face the new troops. The original complement of fifty Spetznas had been eliminated. The onrushing troops threw themselves at the Team members and died in their valiant effort. When there were no more soldiers to fight, the team marched down to the town and found and took out the remaining troops that attempted to hide. Then the entire team moved to the shore where two troop helicopters from the Sword picked them up and ferried them back to the ship.

Later that afternoon Jack and Mark held a team meeting and reviewed the operation. Jack looked over the thirty plus personnel and sighed. "Before any of you tell me how sickening that operation was, I just want you to know how much I agree with you. None of those soldiers or sailors had a chance while we were protected by the force generators. "Fish in a barrel" was an apt term for what we did. But, they deliberately sought to kill all of us and used deception of the highest form to ensnare us and massive overkill to make sure we were dead. It was not our choice that we did not give them a chance. God told the Russian Government not to attack us. In directly defying God they wrote their own troop's death sentence."

There was total silence in the large chow hall they used for team meetings. Jack continued, "Therefore, when the God of the universe expressly told us to destroy these forces to the last fighter we did as we were ordered. When we pray in a few minutes, the Father will remove the feelings of sadness and unfairness from each of us. What He wanted to prove to the Russian troops and the leaders in the Kremlin was that His warriors are invincible and Russia would be foolish to commit more troops to this effort. Personally, I do not know if the leaders will feel overmatched against God. But I also want to remind each of you that God will not be mocked and has a plan for every person killed today. What that is, I do not know but I now clearly understand that death is not an ending but only a step into the next stage of our existence. Thank you, each and every one, for your efforts today and that goes for Captain Conners and his crew of the Sword also. Let us pray. "Dear Heavenly Father ..."

After the team broke up and headed back to their duties, Laura came up to Jack and hugged him. "I feel much better than I did earlier. Still, I hope we don't have to do that again."

Jack smiled, "Me too, but I remember, in the Bible, the masses of His own people, in the thousands, that His people or His angels had to destroy because they disobeyed Him."

CHAPTER THREE

The next day Jack was in prayer during his morning devotional time when he had a visit from Raquel, the Archangel, who appeared in the bedroom in his angelic form and lit up the room. "Greetings Jack Malone, I bring you a message from the Most High. Now hear the Word of God".

"My son, I want you and Mark Connelly to go to the President of Russia and give him this message from me."

"Boris Ubanovitch, you have offended Me twice before the entire world. Therefore, your life is forfeit and I will give your position to another, this month. Your name will be forgotten except as a footnote. My servants have brought you this message so that you can have time to prepare for your end and know that you have not been attacking them, but it is with God that you have chosen to go to war".

"Now, go in My Name and I will be with you."

Raquel had changed into a Crossfire uniform and smiled. "I am going with you. Not as the messenger but as a Heavenly representative to ensure that Satan doesn't get involved in the delivery of this message of God."

When Jack told Mark what had been placed before them, Mark's comment was; "For not working on this level we are certainly getting to meet a lot of Presidents and the like."

Jack nodded in agreement. "What do you think? Something like we did in China?

Mark thought for a few minutes. "No, I think we should do this like we did when we visited the U. S. President, an unexpected, total surprise. That is because this message is a personal one rather than a public one."

Jack thought about it and turned to Raquel who had been uncharacteristically quiet so far. "What do you think, Raquel?"

The Angel smiled, "I've been instructed to follow this time and observe and only make suggestions occasionally. The Most High said that some of your unique solutions could prove highly interesting to the Angels. You two do not follow conventional thinking and your solutions are extremely effective."

Jack laughed, "And sometimes we're extremely outside of the box too."

Even the angel laughed at that. Jack looked at Mark, "I don't think it will be as easy, even invisible, to walk up to the Russian President as it was for the U.S. President. The Russians are a more paranoid than the Americans. We need to plan it a lot tighter. Also, if they have even a thought that we might be calling they will make it very hard to find the President."

Raquel spoke, "It least with me along, you won't have run an ID kit on the man. I can determine if he is the genuine article."

Jack smiled, "Good point, I'll bet we don't even have any access to a sample of his DNA."

Mark laughed, "Don't worry about that. I am sure that the CIA has many samples of his DNA.

Mark called a council meeting of the Core Team for ideas and suggestions. When everyone was there, Mark explained their mission. The first suggestion came from Alexis. "I'd be glad to go with you, I speak flawless Russian and that could be an advantage."

Mark thought about that. "Well, it's a good idea. I do speak some Russian but nobody has ever called it "flawless". Sarah also speaks and writes that language."

David held up his hand, "Me too, and there are a few in the SOG that speak fluent Russian."

The next suggestion came from Charlie Wu. "Why don't you just wing it? They can't stop you or hurt you, if they can detect you."

Jack frowned, "For two reasons Charlie. First, this trip is to announce to a single man his death sentence from God, not to showboat. It requires a sense of decorum. Secondly, this trip we are emissaries of God almighty and we are not going to act zany, which is not what the Crossfire Team is about. A touch of class is required my friend."

Mark added, "Why don't we see if former General Demitri Serakov is available and can give us some insight to our target."

Eight hours later Demitri Serakov stepped out of one of the team's two smallest aircraft, a "Fragment" onto the deck of the Sword and watched as the aircraft was drawn down into the hull of the ship,

Mark had come out to meet him. Demitri exclaimed loud enough to be heard over the sea noise, "Vhere did you get that fantastic aircraft and this awesome ship?"

Mark laughed, "We bought the ship and found the plane in our research division. How are things going for you Demitri?

The big Russian Bear laughed, "I am in high demand by the U.S. Army now that they found out how highly trained I was. They told me that I was helping rewrite the entire book on European warfare. Especially where tanks are concerned."

Mark motioned Demitri inside and followed him into the ship. He led the ex-Russian to their War Room where they met Jack. Demitri gave Jack a big bear hug, "Jack! It's been too long since we destroyed part of a country or even an entire nation, I miss that."

Jack smiled at their old friend that had worked with them on several missions and had even died once with a bullet through his heart defending the team's work in Siberia. God had eliminated that time for everyone so he lived on. "Well this is a message delivery in Moscow, hopefully not a pitched battle. We need to talk to the Russian President."

Demitri frowned a really awesome frown, "Vell, I cannot go with you because they believe I am dead. If dey find out I am not dead, they will correct that mistake. How can I help you otherwise?"

Mark put a map of the Russian Presidential Residence on the table, "We need to make an evening visit to him and thought you could give us an idea on traps, guards, soft spots, and things like that."

Demitri stared at the map and then threw it on the floor. "I could give you good estimates but it would be useless!"

Mark looked from the map on the floor to the man, "Why?"

"That is because he doesn't stay there. He stays in a modest apartment in a Military Base twelve blocks away from that facility. Get me a street map of Moscow and I'll show you.

Mark produced a recent street map of Moscow.

Demitri pointed out the building on the base. "Here he has two thousand soldiers around him and every way to the building is monitored heavily. Dare is no vay you could approach that building without the correct papers and being pre-announced before you show up. Then he probably wouldn't see you anyway." Demitri continued to describe the security measures in place and the guards, snipers, and electronic surveillance that surrounded the President of Russia. He ended with, "But, with God all things are possible. I know in my heart that all of you walk closely with God and you will succeed in your mission."

They said their goodbyes and they prayed for the mission and for Demitri before Mark took him down to the spacious cavern where the aircraft were stored and serviced. Demitri looked around and asked, "How do you fit this huge hanger inside a ship that's not an aircraft carrier?"

Mark laughed, "Demitri; it's all done with mirrors." Mark said with a grin. Demitri boarded the same "Fragment" for his flight back to the U.S.

CHAPTER FOUR

While Jack and Mark discussed their evening trip to Russia, a phone rang in the War Room and Laura answered it. Seeing the phone ID for a call from the U.S. she calculated the time of day for that area code and was on guard. "Good Morning, Crossfire Team, how can we help you?"

The response was faint and somewhat broken up. The woman on the other end of the call sounded upset or frightened. The call floated in and out with Laura getting just about every other word. She spoke up, "Hang on a moment, I'll see if I can improve this call."

Laura used her combat communications system to call Ethan Reaper. "Ethan I've got an international call from Boise, Idaho in the U.S. Can you improve the signal on my line one? I'm only getting every other word."

Ethan locked onto her call and adjusted the volume and clarity by inserting a small delay in the sender's signal, which essentially boosted the signal by compressing the words one at a time. The call was a lot clearer on Laura's end. "There you go, Laura."

Laura thanked Ethan and asked the caller to start over.

The caller identified herself, "Laura, this is Rachel Reynolds, and I need the team's help! I'm on my eighth solo assignment and I've run into something I haven't been trained for, at least, not yet. I've tried to reach Christi but can't reach her."

All this came out in a rush as if time was a precious commodity with little left to waste.

Laura tried to calm Rachel down and ascertain the problem.

In a calm, serious manner, Laura asked, "What is your situation and where are you? Your Area Code indicates you're in Boise, Idaho."

"Yes, you're right, I'm in the Boise Area. My Training Instructor has me following up on a nasty little group that acquires anything for anybody with enough cash. The last three years they've dealt in futures commodity instruments, high-end vehicles, and drug shipment thefts. Six months ago, they upped their operations to a new level, contraband nuclear armaments and stockpiles. Not the military levels, just business commercial stuff, labs and weapons manufacturers. I was tracking them when they moved a major operation to Boise. I believe it is because there was a large shipment of weapons-grade material shipped to a military-contractor here. I'm fairly confident the group wants to steal sufficient quantities of this material to sell to an interested buyer. I also believe it is one that can't get it legally and wanted to use it here in the U.S. That was until last night. I was able to use a laser ear and overheard the leader of this vermin clearly define their target as Israel. He also said they had a way to mask the radiation so that they could get it into Israel without being detected!"

Laura asked her, "Have you informed your Training Instructor of these developments?"

Rachel sounded very focused and mad at the same time. "No! That is one part of the reason I think I need your help. None of my communications methods are functioning! Besides that, I tried to use an open line just to warn them but the calls won't connect. I went to seek assistance from the Israeli government at the closest Consulate, but again, my calls won't go through. I had been given the name and address of a Mossad contact here but they were suddenly killed in a "freak" auto accident last night within an hour after I arranged to meet them. I'm saddened to think I caused them to be killed. I honestly am not even sure why my call to you has gotten through."

Laura asked Rachel, "Have you had any training concerning demons? I understand you had an introduction to one at night when you were with Christi."

Laura could have sworn she could hear Rachel shiver over the phone. "No! That's the part of my training that I haven't had as yet. Do you think that is my problem?"

Laura laughed, "Quite possibly. That sounds like several other operations they have done recently, especially the masking of radiation from nuclear weapons. That's how they were able to sneak a bomb close to Houston and destroy that city."

Laura thought for a few seconds. "Back off from your surveillance of the group and your efforts to spread the news about the operation. It'll be hard to do that but if you don't, they will collect you or kill you very soon. By seeming to give up, they may leave you alone until we can help you. I'll see that the right people are informed. Now, give me your location and a cell phone number I can reach you. I will mention something you and Christi shared recently so you'll know it's me."

Rachel gave her the information and agreed to step down for a while. Before saying goodbye she asked, "Are you and Jack and Christi going to rescue me?"

Laura smiled, "Jack and Christi are on separate missions right now, but you'll get some very good help very soon. Keep praying that God will keep you safe until then."

After breaking off the call, Laura called Sarah, and mether in the War Room. She ran over the conversation she had just finished with Rachel and asked for operational input.

Sarah thought about the situation and prayed for guidance. What she received was quick and expansive. She looked up at her best friend in the world after God and Mark. "God wants us to stop this theft, terminate the thieves, and persuade the demonic to stay out of Rachel's life from now on."

Laura nodded, "That's what I got too. Let's add three more personnel and get an aircraft to sneak into the U.S. post haste. First though, I've got three phone calls to make and I'm going to let you make one"

Four hours later the "Fragment" was approaching Boise in the early afternoon hours, running invisibly and untracked. Besides Laura and Sarah, the craft held David and Alexis and Ethan Reaper as additional forces.

As they prepared to land Sarah asked Laura, "What part of Boise is Rachel in?"

Laura pointed out a hotel off of the Interstate Highway that ran through the area. The hotel was near a major housing development, but sat alone for the present. "This isn't actually Boise, but it's a neighboring community called Meridian. Rach is going to meet us in the mostly empty parking lot to the west of the hotel proper."

After the Fragment landed and everyone disembarked they walked toward the hotel and Rachel met them halfway.

After introductions and hugs, Laura asked Rachel if she had experienced anything new since their talk.

Rachel shook her head. "No, I've just been keeping a low profile like you suggested."

Sarah smiled, "Smart girl! We're here on a three-objective mission from God. First, we have to rescue you. Second, we're to ensure your subject group all get to meet God, and third, We're to train you in demonology 101 and make sure the demons brokering this potential nuclear holocaust never want to cross blades with you again."

Rachel blinked several times as she absorbed the information. "Gee, all I wanted to do was complete my mission and report in."

Laura nodded, "We've notified the U.S. FBI and NSA as to this assault here in Idaho with the objective of destroying Israel with an American bomb. Sarah notified the Israeli Government and the Mossad of your suspicions as to the target and the probability of demonic shielding.

David smiled at the overwhelmed young lady and asked her to show them the probable site for the nuclear theft. She sighed and nodded. "It's about a forty-minute drive to the commercial labs."

While the targeting effort was underway, Ethen had been seeking information on the group involved in the robbery. Rachel told him that they called themselves "The Golden Horde". His computers on the Sword under the control of Charlie's and now Ethan's alter ego "Crayton" begin to amass volumes of data on this present-day version of the 13th century group of Mongols of the same name. But what it revealed made little sense of this supposed operation. Ethan asked "Crayton" if the two stories were at such odds what could it mean?"

The electronic brain of Crayton's immediately coordinated all the facts of the cases and gave Ethan a 97-percent probability in less than 20 seconds.

Ethan checked several sensors of the area they were in and got everybody's complete attention when he spoke loudly. "Folks, this is a demonic trap! It's a total fabrication, designed to draw us in and destroy all of us.

That's why the demons didn't come after Rachel. They were after bigger fish! And, that would be us. Armor up! We've got a couple hundred demons about to spill out of three riffs in less than a minute."

Laura asked him how he had figured it all out.

Ethan smiled, "Because all the members of the recent "Golden Horde" were killed by Russian Special forces two weeks ago trying to steal a suitcase nuke. I saw pictures and IDs on all of the bodies!"

Sarah grabbed Rachel by the arm and ran with her to a point in the parking lot. They stopped and Sarah said "Fragment, Let us in."

Rachel wondered if Sarah had lost it because there was only the two of them, standing there with nothing around them anywhere within earshot.

Then a door slid up in the middle of nothing and a staircase appeared leading up to the open door.

Sarah shoved Rachel up the stairs and into the aircraft. "Stay here. The plane is protected by God's power. The demons cannot get to you as long as you stay inside."

Rachel looked back out of the doorway, "Why doesn't everybody get in here?"

Sarah smiled as she was covered in golden armor and had an awesome sword in her right hand. "Because that would not accomplish our third objective. I'll be back when we're done with these demons." She turned and ran back to the others.

CHAPTER FIVE

Just as Sarah reached the other team members there was a terrible screeching noise as three interdimensional rifts opened around them.

As dozens of different types and forms of demons exited each of the rifts into the human dimension, the bedlam rose in volume exponentially. Screaming, wailing, and grunting, the demons charged into the small group of warriors. Sarah checked and saw that her force generator had a tiny green LED lit showing that it was working. She smiled a smile the demons couldn't understand or want to see.

It was a complete melee as dozens of demons attacked each member of the team, slashing punching and biting to no avail.

Rachel was totally repelled by the hideous demons but greatly encouraged because the demons couldn't seem to hurt the humans. But, that wasn't the case the other way around! She watched as each of the warriors cut a path through the evil hordes. There was a constant fog of smoke around each warrior as demons died and turned into smoke and demon stain. At the rate they were cutting down the numbers, it wouldn't be long before there wouldn't be any demons left.

On the field of battle Laura noticed a rapid dwindling of the number of demons she was contending with at one time. She looked around and saw two of the rifts vanish. A new piece of information opened up in her mind from her time with the Angel Hugo or with the Lord Yahshua. She immediately knew what was happening. She used her combat communications system. "Heads up Crossfire Team, the demons are attempting to nullify our use of the force generators. They are reducing their numbers to our level, which balances our forces. The force generators can only be used to balance greater opposing numbers. Once our forces are equal we won't be able to use the FGs anymore."

Ethan Reaper shrugged his shoulders. "So what? Our armor and swords still give us an equal chance and our training will give us an edge. We can still beat them, one demon at a time."

Laura shook her head, "Satan will start increasing the level of demons we will face until their unrighteousness nullifies our sword's ability to hurt them. It may be only one demon against all five of us, but it can still overcome us one at a time until it exceeds the balance and whoever is left gets their FG back."

Ethan frowned, "Then they will start the dance again."

David said, "Yes they will."

Alexis grinned, "Okay, let us retire to the Fragment so that we can use its field to protect us."

Sarah watched as five upper level demons came out of the remaining rift. "I don't think they are going to allow us to do that."

Alexis hefted her sword into the air. "No problem, you four head over there while I delay this Satanic cannon fodder. Don't worry! Five upper level demons to one of us will most likely give me my FG back."

David looked at his bride, "Not if they only attack you one at a time."

Alexis started bouncing on her feet. "David, please get these three important people I love, and yourself to safety! I've got this." With that, she took off, lightly running toward the approaching demons.

David sighed, "She's right you know. Come on, let's go."

As the four ran to the safety of the shielded aircraft, Alexis tore into the five demons with her uncanny ability to make demons miss her. Sarah looked back and watched as the beautiful blonde danced between the sleek black demons and made them miss with their swords and reduced their numbers with each pass. As the fifth demon lost its head, Alexis took off for the Fragment in a flat-out dash.

All at once, a very-high-level demon materialized between Alexis and the Fragment. Alexis slid to a halt and checked her Force Generator indicator light, it was dark. She looked up at the large demon and realized she wasn't afraid. Even if it killed her, she trusted her God and her Savior. She raised her sword defiantly and smiled at the malevolent creature.

The demon did not understand why this pitiful female was smiling instead of screaming in terror as it raised its huge black sword. "No matter, no power on Earth can save her now!"

His razor-sharp blade raced at the woman's head and she interposed her smaller sword as if it could stop his mighty weapon. To his surprise and dismay, his sword shattered into fragments when it struck the smaller blade with the essence of Yahveh flowing off of it.

He dropped the useless hilt and reached for his target with his left hand. He knew his armor was more than a match for her blade as he waited for her to strike his vulnerable arm. She didn't do it, instead she lowered her blade and fell to one knee with her head bowed. He was about to crush her with one mighty blow when his strength deserted him and he found he couldn't move even a finger. He sensed a powerful presence to his right and looked that way with his eyes. Yahshua walked into the space between the woman and the demon.

"Gf'pokn, why have you defied God and returned to the human dimension after you swore on your life you would never do that again?"

The demon, who was a shredder of souls and a fearful terror pleaded like a child, "My master said it would be all right just this one time so I could do his bidding and destroy these people."

Yahshua looked at the creature with some surprise. "And you believed him?"

"Yes, I wanted to trust him. I should have refused his command."

Yahshua shook his head slightly. "He would have destroyed you if you had refused to do his will. Unfortunately, either way ends your existence. Be gone to the pit to await judgement."

Gf'pokn faded out of sight with a whimper. Yahshua took Alexis' hand and raised her to her feet. "Alexis, you are a rare jewel. Even when you were sure Gf'pokn would surely destroy you, your faith was like a brightly burning flame within you. You conquered all fear and stood against all odds because you trusted me and our Father. Great will be your reward in Heaven. I am proud of you, woman warrior for God." Yahshua disappeared and Alexis walked to the aircraft with a grin on her face.

After being congratulated by the rest of the team, she took David's hand and gently kissed him. "See? I will get to pick out the curtains in our Heavenly mansion."

Everyone relaxed as the Fragment lifted off from the parking lot and invisibly made its way back to the Sword.

Sarah asked Laura, "How are you going to tell Jack about this little trip?"

Maybe I won't bother him with the details like how we got suckered into a trap, again.

Pointing behind himself David asked. "What are we going to do with Rachel?"

Ethan chimed in, "And how are you going to explain the battle in Meridian, Idaho in front of roughly 1,000 cell phone cameras and even more onlookers?"

Laura shook her head, "I'll talk to Jack about all of this.

CHAPTER SIX

The same afternoon that Laura and crew were in Meridian, Idaho, Jack, Mark, and Raquel stepped off of an invisible Fragment onto a second story balcony in Moscow, Russia at eleven o'clock at night. The two men were invisible mode in their Force Generators and Raquel was invisible because he wanted to be that way.

The quiet sounds of the Fragment were totally lost in the roaring and rotor noise of a three-ship flight of Russian Tu-24 war choppers that were returning from a routine nighttime mission. The Fragment moved away from the area and the three of them watched for any sign they had been spotted. Everything settled down with no alarm or outcry.

Mark inspected the three sets of double doors leading to the inside of the building and shook his head. "Well" He spoke quietly into his hush microphone. "It seems I made a mistake. These doors are only ornamental and really not doors at all."

Jack took the news in stride and looked around, "Then first things first. We need to find a way off this balcony and another entry point on the ground floor."

Mark shook his head, which was lost on the others because he was invisible, "Not a good idea, that's where the security is the tightest."

Raquel sighed and took the closer arm of both men and stepped all three of them through the wall to the inside where he released them both.

Jack laughed quietly, "Thanks. Raquel. Now, let's find the Presidential suite." This turned out to be easy because there was only one door with two guards standing in front of it. Raquel rendered the guards not conscious of the three of them entering the suite and closing the door.

Mark said, "You know Raquel, you could have simply transferred us from the Fragment to this room."

Raquel laughed a little laugh, "I suppose I could have, but, where's the fun in that?"

Mark mumbled, "This Archangel is becoming too much like us." He suggested, "Why don't we settle down until Boris shows up?"

Both Jack and Raquel said, "Where's the fun in that?" Mark laughed.

Twenty-five minutes later, Raquel looked at the door. "Boris is in the hall, headed this way and he has company."

A minute later two steely-eyed men entered the room and proceeded to search the rooms very carefully. They were extremely thorough and quick because they knew their lives depended on missing nothing. The two Crossfire warriors and the Archangel moved out of the way if one of the searchers drew close.

As the two men left the rooms, they assured the Russian President that there were no assassins or bombs in the suite of rooms. Boris Ubanovitch walked into the suite escorting a good-looking middle-aged woman dressed in a beautiful ensemble of a golden-hued outfit and darker brown blouse and jacket.

Jack became alert and used his hush mic to talk to Mark, unheard by the couple. "Mark, isn't that the Director of the British Defense Directorate?"

Mark agreed, "It certainly is, this should be interesting", as he prepared to video record the meeting.

Boris spoke excellent English as he had Camilla Albrecht sit down in one of two overstuffed chairs and he sat in the other. "Director Albrecht, have you considered my proposition?"

The British woman calmly studied the Russian President. "Yes I have Mr. President. And I can truly say that it seems workable as well as extremely important for both of our countries."

Boris nodded his head. "Excellent, do you have any questions or reservations at this time?"

She shook her head, "No, some details will need to be finalized just prior to execution of course."

Boris smiled, "But of course. The week before we start I will have my tech people coordinate with your people and arrange for you to watch all phases of the plan through our withdrawal."

Director Albrecht smiled again. "Very well Mr. President, then I shall be on my way." She arose gracefully from her chair and headed for the door to which Boris beat her and opened it for her, "I should be calling you in roughly eight weeks then."

She nodded and left. Boris shut the door and walked back to the sideboard behind his chair and poured himself a generous helping of Vodka in a crystal goblet. Sitting down he took out a cell phone and made a local call. When the other party answered he said, "Ivanovitch! The British are on board and I foresee Mother Russia with all of the warm seaports of France under our control within ninety days. No, I don't see Marco Marino being able to complain about this action without going to war with us, which he dares not do at this time. Anyway it will be an accomplished fact by the time he hears about it." He hung up the call and drained his goblet.

Mark grinned and stored his video camera in a pocket.

The two crossfire warriors switched their force generators to normal and they appeared in the room. Boris was looking the other way and didn't notice them.

As Raquel became visible, Jack stepped over to Boris' side and said, "Mr. President, won't you please join us at the table?"

Boris spun around with fear showing on his face and he raised his free left hand as if to ward off evil spirits. Jack didn't react except to smile and used his right hand to gesture the Russian President to move to the table.

Unsure of how these three people had accessed his domicile he slowly walked over to the table and all four of them sat down.

The Russian President stared at the trio around the table. "Who are you and what do you want? I'm certain that you are not here to assassinate me because you could have easily done that and you haven't."

Causally putting his right hand into the pocket of his jacket, Boris found and depressed the button on the miniature device he found there.

He removed his hand and made a gesture of askance as if to repeat his question silently as he pursed his lips.

Jack smiled at the man to reassure him of their peacefulness, "Mr. President, we are simply messengers and personally we mean you no harm."

Boris nodded, "All right, what is the message and who is it from?"

Jack stared at the man for several seconds. "Before we give you the message I want to put it in the proper prospective. Remember the mass exodus of millions of people from the Earth a little over a year ago? The world hasn't recovered from the effects of that and now we're hearing about thousands of attacks on people all over the world and strange damage to water sources, animals, fish, and vegetation worldwide. What do you believe is behind all these events?"

Boris shrugged his shoulders, "We are not sure but America is blaming the loss of people and the rest of these events on unknown or possibly alien forces. What does that have to do with a message for me?"

Jack sighed, "Mr. President, atheistic belief groups, such as yours here in Russia refuse to consider an all-powerful deity or God. We can show you prophesy that is over two thousand years old that details everything that is going on and what else that will occur before the Son of God returns to rule the Earth in about seven years."

Boris made a sour face. "I've heard all of that talk about an invisible "God" that is the ruler of the world and I don't put any stock in that."

Jack nodded, "That is too bad, Boris because your message is from the God you don't believe in. Now, you can ignore it and consider it foolishness, but it will come true. Now hear the word of the Lord.

"Boris Ubanovitch, you have offended Me twice before the entire world. Therefore, your life is forfeited and I will give your position to another this month. Your name will be forgotten except as a footnote. My servants have brought you this message so that you can have time to prepare for your end and know that you have not been attacking them, but it is with God that you have chosen to go to war."

Jack said, "I'm sorry we had to bring that message to you and ..."

Boris waved him to silence. "Do not worry about it! I'm not worried because I know it is not true. There is no "all-knowing" God or angels or demons. These are things that man made up at the beginning of time so that they would feel better and more in control. The real questions are; how did you get in here? And, what I am going to do with you now that you are here?"

Mark spoke for the first time. "Boris, we got in here through the power of the God you don't believe in and we will leave the same way. You and your whole military cannot hurt us and I don't recommend you try."

Boris spoke into the air, "Now!"

Nothing happened. Boris got up and went to the door and opened it. There were no guards outside the door in the silent hall. He turned around in confusion. "There should be a hundred troops out here."

Raquel quietly said, "Because you activated the little alarm button in your jacket pocket? I altered the signal to one that told everyone to leave and to not interrupt you."

Boris stared at Raquel for several seconds. "I don't believe you. You never moved since we sat down."

Raquel considered the man coolly. "Mr. President, I have been to three other dimensions and six other places on Earth since we sat down. I am not a human being like you, I am an Angel of God and am not restrained to three dimensions nor time as you are."

Boris looked like he wanted to laugh at the words of Raquel but wasn't sure he should.

Raquel stood up and changed into his Archangel persona. His radiant arraignment lit up the room and the golden-handled sword by his side added emphasis to his image.

Raquel disappeared from sight. Jack looked at the door to see how Boris was taking this but he was gone also.

Mark sighed, "The Russian President is getting one of Raquel's explicit tours of Heaven and Hell. You know he will probably be a believer when he returns. Think that will save him?"

It was Jack's turn to shrug his shoulders, "I'm not the judge of that, thank God." He got up and went to close the door.

CHAPTER SEVEN

Raquel and Boris returned to the room suddenly. The Archangel showed no expression but the Russian President was a basket case. His face was infused with blood so that it looked bright red. He had been sweating profusely and his shirt was soaked. The pupils were small in his wide-open eyes, a sure sign of having been terrorized. His breathing was rapid and shallow, a sign of shock. He was shaking uncontrollably and rapidly glancing around in obvious fear for his life.

Jack took the man's arm, led him to a large, overstuffed chair, and got him to sit down. Mark brought him a large glass tumbler full of liquid and Boris almost drained it in three gulps. He made a big sigh and started to calm down. Jack looked at Mark, "Good idea to give him some water."

Mark snorted, "Water my foot, that was 150-proof Vodka!"

Boris' eyes looked much more normal and he had ceased shaking. Still, he grabbed Jack's hand and almost pleaded, "I didn't know! I can't go back there! Please help me."

Jack had been praying silently ever since Boris had disappeared. Following the leading he had received, he led the former-atheist in a salvation prayer to Yahshua. He left Boris in desperate tears and sobbing and walked over to Raquel. "Was this part of God's plan?"

The Archangel nodded his head. "One of several possibilities. You realize that by accepting Christ he will lose his position and everything he has here on Earth. But, his confession was true so he won't go to hell. But, it will be a rough time for him until his end. Remember Revelation 9:3 - 9:5? "

"And he opened the bottomless pit, and there arose a smoke out of the pit, as the smoke of a great furnace; and the sun and the air were darkened by reason of the smoke of the pit. And out of the smoke came forth locusts upon the earth, and power was given them, as the scorpions of

the earth have power. They were told not to hurt the grass of the earth, nor any green thing, nor any tree, but only the men who do not have the seal of God on their foreheads. And they were not permitted to kill anyone, but to torment for five months; and their torment was like the torment of a scorpion when it stings a man. And in those days shall men seek death, and shall not find it; and shall desire to die, and death shall flee from them."

"Boris now knows the truth, and the truth he knows will set him free. But, during the remainder of his time here, he still has to reap the harvest of things he has planted already."

Jack and Mark consoled Boris and prayed for peace for him. They then disappeared and walked out of the building and avoided the guards and the gates until they found an open lot where they boarded the invisible "Fragment" and returned to the Sword.

After filling out their after-action reports and summarizing the mission to the Core Team they got some time off. Jack was relaxing on a couch in the living room of his apartment suite when the Team Call Emergency alarm sounded throughout the "C" compartment of the Sword. Jumping to his feet, he called Mark on his battle-com system. "What's the alarm for, Mark?"

Mark replied, "I don't know. I'm headed for the War Room right now."

Laura suddenly ran into the bedroom, "Something sounds like it's definitely urgent."

Jack raised an eyebrow. "Where are you coming from? I thought you were asleep in the bedroom."

She smiled, "A separate mission. I'll tell you all about it later, after we settle whatever this alarm is about."

There was no sense of worry or undue concern shown by any of the team members they encountered on their run to the War Room, just efficient movement to duty stations by men and women dressed and armed for war.

Upon reaching the entrance to the War Room, Jack and Laura walked to their seats and sat down just as the alarm quit sounding. Jack looked around at the rest of the Core Team. "Who called the alert?"

Ethan Reaper's voice responded in the air, "I sounded the alarm General Malone. I have detected multiple physical assaults aimed at the Sword from the outside while we are at speed. These attacks have been ineffectual due to the Force Generator field but are continuing to increase in number and ferocity and they have serious demonic spiritual attributes that are becoming noticeable on my sensor arrays. I'm not positive, but I believe these are the demonic spirits released from the abyss as described in Revelations 9:3 through 9:5."

Christi asked, "I think those passages apply to a different event. Because, I believe those demons aren't released from the abyss until after the fifth seal was opened and that's not supposed to happen until the second half of the Tribulations. Aren't we only in the first year of the seven years of the Tribulations?"

Laura had been praying over this question when information planted in her mind opened up. She spoke up. "Ethan is mixing up Tribulation events. These are demons in physical form that Satan has attacking people all over the world but, they are not the horse-sized demons of Revelation 9. That would mean the other Seal judgments would have already occurred, which they haven't as yet. This is simply a foretaste of things to come. The enemy is using these demons to frighten people that did not go in the rapture in an attempt to keep them from finding and embracing Yahshua and through Him, Yahveh God."

David asked, "Shall we pray and seek Heaven's guidance as to our response to these attackers?"

Everyone agreed and Jack led them in prayer. "Yahshua, we adore You and everything You do for us. We speak and sing praises to Your name in everything we do. We come seeking Your guidance as to this team's efforts to counter this demonic effort against Your believers. Your love and protection keeps us safe from their attacks Lord. What would you have us do to help others?"

The heaviness Jack associated with the presence of God's Holy Spirit settled over the team members and peace filled them all. There was a disturbance in the air in the middle of the room that quickly resolved into a whirling mass of gold and white. The Angel Rose was suddenly among them.

Jack looked into her eyes and realized the wisdom of eternity was looking back at him. Rose smiled, "Warriors

all, the Most High has heard your prayers and I have been honored to bring you His answer. *"Your team is not to be concerned with this activity of Satan. The demons attacking you will soon realize the futility of their efforts and will look for other targets. The Most High will attend to them. Your challenge will be to*
respond to the oncoming attacks against your team by the military of Russia and the Anti-Christ."

Rose continued, "Your presence in the Russian President's residence has become known and their government has determined you were the cause for Boris' mental collapse which made him unfit to hold his position any longer. They were given this information by Marco Marino who received it from the agents of Satan."

Rose rotated in the air and looked at all the Core Team members. "As with the Chinese, ignore these attacks unless it could cause death or destruction to innocents not involved in your struggles. Pray continuously and be of good faith because God is with you, as are we."

The Angel faded out of sight with her signature swirling of colors.

Jack prayed their thanks to a loving Father for the message and the messenger. "Okay folks, let's go on a war footing as of now and prepare for these attacks."

CHAPTER EIGHT

Ethan Reaper had been an exceptionally good hacker before being hired into the Crossfire Team. While he had become a trustworthy leader and warrior for the team, he hadn't forgotten his earlier talents. Of course, now he used those talents to help the team.

Ethan was using the Crossfire Team's array of highly advanced CRAY Computers to ease his way into the software for the planning echelon for the Russian military. He knew he couldn't sneak into the actual military files as they were too protected against outside penetration. So he elected to hack into the inter-departmental email communications and see if he could get any information on their plans to attack the Crossfire Team. He had been rewarded beyond his wildest hopes and had just backed out of the Russian systems and summed up his research.

He paged Jack Malone and Mark Connelly and requested they come to his office in COMM/SEC. They walked into Ethan's office and Mark asked what Ethan had discovered.

"Either some very skillful misinformation or some pretty scary stuff. Assuming this info is real, then the Russians are about to dance with the devil and fan the flames of a possible world-wide nuclear war simply to destroy us."

Jack glanced at Mark and an unspoken message passed between them. "Run it down for us Major Reaper."

Ethan nodded and scanned his summary. "Our present course is going to take us near the home island of Japan in the next twelve hours. The Russians are taking a page out of our combat book and will try to disintegrate the Sword using their version of "Rods of God" when we are less than fifty miles from Japan. Then, if that doesn't work they plan to overwhelm us with ten simultaneous nuclear weapon strikes fired from ten different stealth aircraft all illegally flying within the airspace of Japan."

Jack shook his head. "We know that these efforts will not destroy us, but they could easily kill thousands of

Japanese. God told us to fight back to prevent damage to innocents. What do you think will prevent the Japanese damage that could be caused by these attacks and discourage the Russians sufficiently to put an end to these irresponsible attacks for once and forever?"

Mark had spent several hours praying to God concerning this very thing. "I'll tell you what God told me around four A.M. this morning. We are to reduce the Russian capability to wage war at such a rate they will sue for peace to prevent becoming a first-world power with only a fourth-world military. This means existing equipment, manufacturing capabilities, command and control facilities, missile storage areas, standing armies, and the military hierarchy. Big country but, God said he would give us the victory."

Jack's heart felt cold concerning the death they would have to deal out. He prayed that the Father would give him peace over this action because he knew that God didn't make mistakes and if this was God's Will, Jack knew he and the team would do it.

With a wave of peace came a Word from God. *"My child, as your team begins to reduce their military capability, the Russians will understand very quickly and hasten to make a lasting pact with your team to leave each other alone. They will keep their word this time. These present attacks are actually the work of an extremist faction of their government who will be "removed" for their stupidity in ordering these attacks. I will have Raquel show them what the extent of their losses will be. I will be with you as you show them that I cannot be beaten."*

Jack prayed his thanks to God. Turning to Ethan he grinned a grin that bothered the young Major on several levels. "We will take the Rod attack but, I want the ten stealth aircraft destroyed before they release their nuclear weapons. Figure out how to do that, quickly!"

Ethan immediately called Captain Robert Maxwell out of his training class to help him with the problem. Rob walked in and sat down in the COMM/SEC office. "What can I do for you Major?"

Ethan grinned, "First, just call me Ethan. Second, I need your help with an air defense issue. I need a solution on how to destroy ten separate latest-generation stealth fighters in the air, coming in multiple different directions at multiple Mach speeds, before they can simultaneously unleash their nuclear weapons."

Rob smiled, "Oh good, nothing too serious then?"

Ethan made a face showing his irritation concerning the Captain's answer.

Rob shook his head, "Levity a little too much? What nation is supplying these fighters?"

"Russia is the supplier and the attacker."

Rob thought for a moment, "Then, they will probably be PAC-FAs and we can take them fairly easily."

Seeing the doubtful look on Ethan's face Rob continued, "The PAK-FA is equipped with L-band radar arrays, which are able to detect the presence of a fighter-sized stealth aircraft. While the L-band radar doesn't allow the PAK-FA to target a stealth aircraft, it does allow the pilot to focus the jet's other sensors on a particular area of the sky. That's where we can defeat them."

" How?"

"Over the last two years our developmental group has been secretly creating a new class of drones called "Hellethal". These are very thin with no wings because they are lifting surfaces themselves. A Hellethal drone is a hyper-speed transport designed to deliver two to four Hellethal hyper-speed air-to-air missiles, which were specifically created to locate, lock on, and to totally destroy stealth fighter jets. Because of the hyper-speed transport's minimal cross-section, it is completely invisible to L-band radar. We have five of these systems in the inventory here on the Sword. Each one can take out three to four of the PAK-FAs."

Ethan sighed, "Thank you Yahshua!"

CHAPTER NINE

Ethan called Jack and Mark back to his office. "Captain Maxwellhere has a solution to our irresponsible Russian stealth fighters."

Rob explained everything to the two team leaders. Mark asked, "If the drone is so small, how big are the missiles?"

"They are eight feet long and two feet in diameter. Before you determine that isn't large enough to carry propulsion fuel and explosives I'll tell you they don't. These missiles don't use explosives. They are a cross between a rail gun and Rods from God. Only fired horizontally rather than dropped vertically."

"The projectile is fired from the drone using an electric charge of 10.6 mega joules, that's a one second pulse of 10.6 million watts, or enough electricity to power the average American household for a year. When applied in a single split second to an alloy rod that's much, much smaller than your house, it's enough to make the rod accelerate to Mach 7. Conceive of something moving fast enough to ignite the air around it and to destroy anything it strikes in ways science barely understands. The brute force of a two-kilogram rod traveling over 5,000 miles per hour makes them ideal for totally destroying stealth fighter planes before they know they've been targeted. Targeting is a visual thing with no radar to warn the target."

Mark was impressed. "Make it happen tomorrow morning right after they try to destroy us with their kinetic weapon."

Jack asked, "Can you guarantee that you can locate, track, and destroy all ten of these independent stealth fighters?"

Rob nodded his head. "Actually, it will be relatively simple."

Ethan asked, "What about the nuclear missiles that they will be prepared to fire? Will they detonate?"

Rob thought for a bit. "That's a lot more hypothetical since we've never done that before. The force involved in the kinetic strike should fragment their missiles and prevent detonation. We need to seek God's help as to any possible deviations."

Mark nodded, "Even if they do explode they should be sufficiently high enough and far enough away from the Japanese mainland to minimize casualties."

Rob agreed and set to work preparing the drones.

As the Sword approached the location nearest to Japan everyone's nerves were on edge. The ship was running on the surface on full alert when Rob notified them that the American satellite he was stealing data from had identified the locations of the ten Russian stealth aircraft closing in on the ship at Mach 2 from five different directions.

Mark told Rob "Hold fire until we're attacked. We don't want to be the aggressors due to bad Intel."

The Sword's Executive Officer, Hugh Kelly announced, "There are two Japanese warships headed toward the Sword on a non-aggressive course and are openly hailing us to heave to for inspection. And get this, there is an American destroyer accompanying the Japanese ships."

Jack shook his head, "Warn them off, tell them we're monitoring Russian jets on a nuclear attack course for our ship at this moment!"

Hugh sent the message and the three oncoming ships hastily altered course away from the Sword.

Ethan hit the collision alarm and the alarm tones were heard throughout the ship seconds before the Russian "Rod" from space slammed into the Force Generator field. Traveling at over five thousand miles per hour the hundred-kilogram rod was carrying a tremendous amount of kinetic energy. Mark told Rob, "Take out the fighters, now!"

The Force Generator field absorbed the energy from the kinetic weapon without problem. Ten Hellethal air-to-air missiles struck all ten of the fighter jets at over five thousand miles per hour and obliterated the ten aircraft, which had, themselves, been traveling at Mach 2 speeds.

The expanding spheres of energy overlapped and smashed into the Sea of Japan causing the shipping in the area to have control issues as the waters suddenly became energized into whitecap waves up to ten feet in height.

Ships from dinghies to capitol vessels were thrown around and shook up, some of the smaller ones were slightly damaged, but none were lost.

When things had settled down, Jack had the XO contact the American and Japanese ships and offer to meet with them.

Escorting the visiting officers to the conference room Jack explained what just occurred. He backed up his comments with videos and radar plots. In slow motion he showed the last microseconds of the falling Rod from above and in one case, the end of one of the Russian stealth jets. Fielding their questions, he explained their mission and God's protection for the Sword and the team. When they had resolved the attacks and their defenses, Jack declined to give them a tour of the ship due to critical operations involving additional attacks by the Russians that could be compromised at that time.

After the Japanese had returned to their ships Mark escorted the American group to the deck. The XO from the American ship asked Mark one last question. "General Connelly, regardless of your dislike of the present government in the U.S. how can you justify keeping such technology from the soldiers and sailors you used to serve with? Knowing that this advanced technology could save their lives?"

Mark studied the man for several seconds. "Three simple reasons Commander. First, it is not mine to give or keep from anyone. These "technologies" belong to God and He determines who uses them. Second, if I could make them available to others, I would give them only to the forces or people that God tells me to give them to. And lastly, I would want to end war and evil on the Earth but it is already arranged to end those things in about seven years when Yahshua, or Jesus as you know Him returns to reign and rule the Earth for a thousand years."

Seeing the look of skepticism on the man's face Mark asked innocently, "Would you like some in controversial proof of that?"

Believing he had Mark in an unprovable position the Commander smiled, "I definitely would."

Mark spoke into the air, "Raquel".

The Archangel appeared next to Mark in his Archangel motif and said, "Yes Mark Connelly, what can this servant of the Most High God accomplish for you today?"

The scene was almost surreal with the sun shining brightly and the sea off the Japanese main island, calm and vast with only a slight breeze to cool the heat of the day and a seven-foot tall Angel of God coolly appraising the naval commander and his three men.

Mark smiled, "It seems our Commander here has a belief problem concerning the return of the Messiah to Earth in the next six plus years. Would you do me the favor of letting him see his possible futures and how they will affect him?"

One of the Seaman ratings didn't look like he wanted anything to happen to his officer and put his hand on the butt of his service weapon. Mark tipped his head to the side, "Oh, why don't you include the Commander's security group too?"

Raquel and the four men suddenly vanished from the deck. Mark walked over to the base of the command tower on the deck of the Sword and sat down on the deck to await their return.

Eighteen minutes later the same group returned. From the look on the Commander's face and those of his men, doubt about their choices concerning God, Heaven, and Hell were no longer a subjective matter.

Mark stood up, took the Commander's right hand, and shook it. "I hope that helps clarify things about your futures when the Messiah returns to Jerusalem. Good day gentlemen."

The deck crew of the Sword had to assist the four men in getting into their lighter without falling overboard, they also made sure that they were headed in the right direction to make the short trip back to their ship.

Jack was in the War Room looking at the developing plan for reduction of Russia's military when Raquel appeared next to him. Jack smiled, "Hello, Heavenly warrior, how goes the battle?"

Raquel laughed, "As usual, except for your team. Do you know that I really enjoy my trips here because each of you are attempting to walk a holy life as we angels do, but, somehow, you always find some humor in your lives?"

Jack looked questioningly at the Archangel. "What have we done to amuse you this time?"

"Mark had me give some of your guests a quick tour of their choices between Heaven and Hell. One of the men, while quite shaken, stated that Heaven looked wonderful but he didn't like Hell because it reminded him somewhat of a bad day at his human home here on Earth. Considering the seriousness of what they saw I would say that's funny!"

CHAPTER TEN

The next morning Mark received a call from Vice Admiral Cooper of the U.S. Navy. Although Mark had never met the man himself, the Admiral's credentials spoke highly of his service history, as did everyone that knew about him. Tough as nails, dedicated to the navy before anything else in his life. Rumors had been floating about for the last year that Cooper was a shoo-in as the next Admiral of the Navy. From what Mark knew of the man he was an honorable and very efficient officer who deserved promotion to that position.

"Yes Sir, Admiral Cooper, how can the Crossfire Team help you?"

Admiral Cooper's voice was loaded with command overtones but he still came across simply as one military man to another. "General Connelly, if it is possible, I would like you and your wife to attend a private luncheon with me today aboard the G.W. Bush, at two bells of the afternoon watch. We've got some things to discuss that I think you'll find interesting and important."

Mark didn't think about it. The Holy Spirit was almost shouting that God was very much in favor of this meeting. "We'll be there Admiral."

After discussing the meeting with Jack, Laura, and the rest of the Core Team, Mark and Sarah put on their dress uniforms, which included their ranks. As a two-star Israeli Airforce General Mark was technically in charge of his one-star General wife. He knew better than anyone that Sarah accepted his higher rank and let him keep it. They arrived in one of the "Fragments" from the research group now known as The Crossfire Air Force.

Stepping out onto the deck of the newly commissioned G.W. Bush they were met by the Admiral and a complete Welcoming ceremony including a brass band. Awed and a little humbled, the two Crossfire Team leaders returned the salutes and inspected the troops lined up on the deck before being ushered into the Admiral's private quarters for an excellent lunch. Finally, they got to sit down with the Admiral and talk.

Admiral Cooper held up two bulky files and smiled at them. "I took the liberty of researching both of you and your individual careers and your more recent encounters with notoriety. I don't normally commend people but in your cases I am impressed. Also, since both of you have had extensive training and service in your military careers I believe you understand honor on the battlefield." The Admiral smiled, "And you've both seen more action in the last five years than most have. I need to tell you that this meeting and whatever comes out of it is completely unsanctioned and is not approved by my superiors in our civilian government. You can honestly say I am "sort of" committing treason by meeting with you two, or any representative of the Crossfire Team."

Sarah smiled at the Admiral, "Sir, why do you say, "sort of instead of just admitting it?"

Admiral Cooper studied the two people in front of him. He obviously came to a conclusion that meant a lot to him. "Because I am only a single member of an immense, and growing, number of American military personnel who have come to the same conclusion that you and your team mate, Jack Malone, spelled out to us over a year ago, that our government officials have sold our country out to a foreign power."

Mark noted that the Admiral didn't try to pretend he would deny he ever said anything to them about this. This spoke volumes to Mark about this man's integrity and his personal code of honor.

The Admiral continued, "The President and his followers have broken their oaths they swore to uphold the Constitution of the United States of America and to protect the country from all enemies, foreign or domestic. They are attempting to put the U.S. Military under the control of the New World Government headed by Marco Marino. Since we are the ones that would enforce that order, it isn't really happening. It's a lot like the excuse you gave during that terrorist attack on that Zim Lines Israel liner when you were ordered to stand down. Somehow the chopper's radio ceased to function."

Mark laughed, "Gee Admiral, I didn't realize my act of insubordination had reached your level."

"Back then I wasn't an Admiral, I was the Commander of the set of ships you SEALs were working out of. The only reasons I didn't bust you down to Seaman No Class were the fact that you made it work and saved those people, and it was exactly what I would have done if I was in your shoes at the time."

Sarah asked, "Admiral, you're walking a very fine line on this. If the government has any inkling of your divided loyalties, they will probably have you killed and scatter or destroy all the troops under your command."

The Admiral nodded his head. "I, and others, are aware of these possibilities. That's why I wanted to speak to you off the record. Actually, at this moment I am giving a speech in Washington. We have the most sophisticated military in the world and what I want your team to be aware of is, that if we are forced to attack you, it won't happen. It may look like it will, but I can assure you that the men and women of the branches of the U.S. Military are on your side while looking very different. These Navy, Air Force, Army, Marines, and Coast Guard people are acutely aware that your team is commanded and protected by God. That's why we will throw bombs and missiles your way. But you have proved to us, and we know, they won't affect you. Try to ignore us, please."

Mark prayed for God's confirmation of what the Admiral was proposing and felt God's concurrence. He looked at the Admiral. "You've got a deal. Please realize that even though the Russians don't believe in God, we wouldn't have killed those ten pilots if they hadn't threatened innocents using their nuclear missiles so near to Japan. Their missiles would not have bothered us."

The Admiral grinned, "We'll see that innocents aren't in danger if we're forced to attack you. So, nuclear weapons don't worry you while you're in your ship?"

Sarah laughed, "Admiral, Mark and Jack were floating only twenty-five feet away from two One Mega-ton warheads when they detonated. You need to remember that God created everything in the Universe simply by speaking it into existence. Bombs have no power over Him and those He protects."

The Admiral agreed and stood up. Mark stood and shook the man's hand. "Admiral, the world needs more leaders like you. I pray that God calls you into relation with His Son, Yahshua."

As he walked them back to their aircraft the Admiral shrugged his shoulders, "I'm pretty sure that's coming soon, I just found out by DNA testing that I'm actually Jewish."

As the Fragment prepared to leave the Deck of the G.W. Bush, Sarah got a word from God. "Aircraft! Do not take off! Open the hatch, Now!" She looked at Mark, "Come on." She jumped off of the steps and ran back over to the Admiral.

The Admiral was confused by their sudden return. "What's the problem?"

Sarah put her right hand on the officer's shoulder and looked him in the eyes. "Admiral, I just got a word from God about you. If you have a backup plan to replace you in your duties here, you need to do it right now."

The Admiral looked around. Seeing nothing out of the ordinary he asked "Why?"

Mark had been praying and received the same word as Sarah had. "Because Admiral, there are two components to everything that happens on Earth. The natural and the spiritual. Apparently, in the spiritual, Satan just found out you have Jewish ancestry and that you are working with us."

Mark could feel the spiritual balance tilting. "Stay with Sarah and I while we get you onto the Fragment! Order your men to clear this part of the deck ASAP! We've got demons coming with orders from Marco Marino to kill you. Your weapons won't hurt them, but ours will!"

As the Admiral cleared the deck, two Marines assigned to protect the Admiral wouldn't leave his side. God let Mark and Sarah know that both men were trustworthy.

Mark took a stand on the wind-swept deck of the Navy battle cruiser and faced into the wind as he could feel the approaching demonic forces. He started praying in his prayer language but his sword and armor didn't appear, yet.

Sarah got the Admiral and the two Marines into the Fragment, which was protected by a Force Generator field.

She turned and sternly told all three men, "Do not leave this aircraft! These demons can't get to you in here, but outside this door they will kill you. You guys are already heroes in our book, you don't need to prove it to anyone." She jumped out of the aircraft and ran over to stand next to Mark.

Mark said loudly, "Raquel! I feel we're going to need your help here."

Raquel appeared in his Angelic form next to Mark. "Just waiting until you asked for help. You are very right about your needing help, so I brought along some friends."

Mark looked behind them and saw about thirty of the Heavenly Host arrayed around the deck behind the three of them with their swords drawn. Sarah said, "Here we go, Armor up!"

CHAPTER ELEVEN

On the Fragment the two Marines had been asking that the Admiral allow them to go outside and fight like Marines to help in the battle to come. Admiral Cooper got upset and said, "Stand Down! That woman who told you to stay in here is a one-star General in the Israeli Air Force and I believe she knows exactly what is coming and that she knows it is more than we can handle!"

On the deck as they prayed strongly, both Mark and Sarah's armor and swords exploded into bright visibility. A hundred feet from their positions a major rift in space between the demonic world and the human dimension opened and at least two hundred demons of every shape and size came boiling out onto the deck of the ship. A somewhat humorous note was that the bottom of the rift was about three feet too high and most of the demons stumbled out and fell into clumps on the deck until they got themselves sorted out. That really angered the demons even more than normal and they were a violent group to start with.

With a tremendous crash the line of demons slammed into the line of humans and angels. Mark saw there wasn't going to be any finesse in these battles. It was simply sword, claw, and fang against swords and armor everywhere you looked. He muscled through the defenses of many demons and dispatched them as efficiently as he could. He still had to be careful because neither he nor Sarah had the protection of a Force Generator field at this point.

The Lord used the fields to balance out the enemy's numerical advantages and right now, with thirty Angels and an Archangel there wasn't enough of an imbalance to warrant the use of the fields for the two humans.

Several demons saw Mark and changed direction so that they might defeat him specifically. Mark was sure Satan still had a bounty out on his head. He matched Sarah as they both went into the time-compression technique they had learned from the training Angel, Hugo. Mark was able to take out sixteen different demons before dropping back to normal speed and breathing hard. He glanced around and could see all of the Heavenly Host of Angels were wholly involved in combat and still, the number of demons flowing out of the demonic rift was still increasing and the tide of battle was swinging their way with four or five demons for every defender.

On the Fragment the two Marines no longer had any interest in attempting to get out of the safety and join the battle. This was the first time either man had seen a single demon, let alone dozens of horrible types. The unrelenting hatred and mindless violence toward them was overwhelming.

The demons trying to get into the plane were extremely vile and way past ugly. Frustrated by the Force Generator field they even turned to killing other demons that interfered with their attacks. They tended to hack or club a lesser demon to death and weren't shy about what they did with the corpses.

One Marine mumbled, "I think we'd better not go against that Israeli General's order to stay here."

An upper level demon emerged out of the rift and attacked Sarah. She outmaneuvered the demon and chopped her sword down on the large demon's neck. Her sword bounced off and the demon used its left hand to deliver a massive blow to Sarah's chest. As she flew backward to collapse onto the deck, her armor and sword disappeared.

The Admiral was sickened in his spirit by the evil hordes and in his revulsion he prayed that God would destroy the attackers and save the defenders. For a man who wasn't sure of his belief in God ten minutes ago, this was a very fervent prayer.

Raquel was slaying demons at a great rate when God spoke to him. He raised his sword on high and spoke a Heavenly power word with such volume that the entire Battle Cruiser vibrated strongly. Rippling away from Raquel in all directions, the word disintegrated all of the demons it touched instantly including the higher-level demon.

In less than twenty seconds the ship was empty of anything demonic and the rift imploded into nothingness. Everyone on the ship was strongly convicted of the truth and reality of both Yahveh God and His Son, Yahshua in that instant. There was no doubt or confusion as to the Messiah and the truth of his message.

Mark sighed as the demons disappeared and slumped to his knees on the deck of the ship in a fog of complete exhaustion. His armor and sword vanished and he looked around for Sarah.

He saw her collapsed on the deck without her armor or sword. His love for her and his concern overcame his tiredness and he struggled to his feet, He went over to her praying that Yahshua would tend to her injuries.

His spirit sagged within him when he realized that she was truly dead. He dropped to his knees and gathered her limp body in his arms. The pain he felt hurt so much it overwhelmed his ability to reason. Hardheaded as he tended to be, he had learned of their total dependence on God through years of spiritual combat. So his prayer was one of love and gratitude to a loving Father he knew could restore his dead wife to him. He knew in his heart that she was going to be in Heaven when it was her time and things could not be better for her. That made him realize that all the pain he was feeling was for himself if he lost Sarah.

Sarah was like an empty vessel with no tension in her body and no pulse or breath. But, the pain in his heart eased knowing she was in the Father's hands. He clung to her motionless body and the tears ran down his face as he stared at the possibility of her loss and that hurt was more than he could bear.

When all the Angels, other than Raquel, had disappeared, the Admiral had gotten out of the plane and now he stood by Mark. He felt Mark's pain and his own tears freely ran down his face at the loss of Sarah. He put his hand on Mark's shoulder in a sign of sympathy for his loss.

Raquel knelt down beside Mark and when Mark looked into the Archangel's eyes he saw the Father's love and compassion staring back at him. Raquel gathered up both Mark and Sarah in his arms and they vanished.

The Admiral stood alone on the deck of the ship and felt the weight of responsibility for her death because she had given her life defending him. He didn't know what to do because he was sure that Satan would come at him again and he was alone now.

He felt some very powerful vibrations and looked up with flash of fear only to see a much larger advanced aircraft settling to the deck near him. The hatch opened on the side of the "Formidable" and six people disembarked. A tall man and woman walked over and saluted the Admiral. Admiral Cooper recognized Jack Malone and his wife Laura from the files he had studied on the Crossfire Team. He returned their salutes and used his left hand to scrub at the tears on his face. He was surprised that the one, over-riding emotion that he felt was relief that there was still hope for himself because he recognized that these were more warriors in the same mold as Mark and Sarah Connelly. The Admiral held out his hand. "Welcome aboard, I wish I had better news but the devil sent hundreds of his demons to kill me and in the battle, Mark's wife Sarah was killed helping to defend me."

Laura stepped over to the Admiral and put her hand on his shoulder at the same time that Jack took the Admiral's arm in his grasp. The spiritual anointing, they carried staggered the naval officer. A deep peace surged through his mind and body as Jack and Laura prayed for him to receive God's peace and understanding.

The Admiral felt the weight of concern for Sarah fade away. He looked at the couple. "I suddenly don't seem too bothered by Sarah's death."

CHAPTER TWELVE

Mark was having trouble keeping his wits about him because of his utter exhaustion from both the high speed combat and the non-stop fighting with demons for the entire battle on the ship, and because he was deeply saddened about losing Sarah.

Raquel had brought them to a room somewhere in the third heaven. The Archangel had lain Sarah's body on a soft, flat surface and then turned to Mark. Raquel placed his hand on Mark's arm and smiled at him. Mark felt the strangest sensation he'd ever had. He felt the exhaustion, the aches, and the tiredness simply drain away from his body like water drains out of a bathtub. Filling up the empty place that the spent feelings left was a high level of energy and optimism. He smiled back at his large spiritual friend and turned to look at Sarah's body lying on the couch, table, whatever it was. She was almost puddled onto the surface with no tension showing in any of her muscles. He turned to Raquel to find him down on one knee with his head bowed.

Mark copied the Angel and quickly knelt next to him on the floor. He felt the energy level on the room climb quickly and heard Yahshua's voice say, "Rise warriors."

As they stood up, the Son of God smiled at them and Mark's spirit lit up as his heart rejoiced in the Messiah's closeness. Yahshua went over to the surface Sarah's body was on and sat on the edge of it. He straightened some strands of her hair as he smiled at her. He placed His hand on her shoulder as he said, "You have done well, my good and faithful servant, Rise and shine again in the world below for a brief time until we all meet again."

To Mark it was like watching her body fill up with life and energy and become animated. She opened her beautiful brown eyes and smiled at her Savior. She lithely rose up into a kneeling position, took Yahshua's hand and tenderly kissed it.

Yahshua patted her arm gently and then faded from sight. Sarah looked up and saw Mark. She grinned the biggest grin he'd ever seen and hopped off the surface to walk over to him and embraced him like it was to be forever.

Mark hung onto her like he would never let her go again. He didn't say a word but expressed all of his love and appreciation in his physical nearness to her.

After a bit Sarah stepped back and held Mark at arm's length and looked him over. "I missed you."

That caused Mark to release all of his pent up worry and fears for her in laughter. He hugged her again, and whispered in her ear, "Please, please, try real hard to never, ever leave me again."

She nodded her head, too overcome with emotion to trust her words to convey her agreement to his request and her love for him. She held him as tightly as she could to send a positive signal of eternal love that he would never forget.

After several minutes, Raquel asked, "Are you ready to return?"

Sarah nodded and Mark said quietly, "Make it so, Raquel."

They suddenly found themselves back on the deck of the G.W. Bush near Jack, Laura, and Admiral Cooper. David and Alexis were standing with Ethan and Christi next to the Formidable.

Everyone gathered around Sarah and expressed their happiness at her return.

Mark looked at the Admiral. "Sir, I want to apologize for my behavior after the battle and ask that you forgive me for the lack of decorum."

The Admiral shook his head, "Don't worry about that. After seeing what you, Sarah, and the angels did to those things Satan sent to kill me I don't think it matters. What am I to do now?"

Laura smiled, "Why don't we ask the God of the universe what He wants you to do. I doubt that the Anti-Christ or the present administration will allow a "Jew" to stay in command very long."

The team stood in a circle on the Battle-Cruiser's deck and bowed their heads as they sought guidance from the

Creator of the Universe. Alexis began to sing softly about "nothing but the blood of Jesus" a song she had loved ever since she first learned it as a child. The others joined in with a joyous chorus and soon it was being sung by many of the sailors and Marines on the deck. The song grew in volume and timber as other voices added their heartfelt belief in the Messiah and His gift to all men and women.

Suddenly, with a flash of gold on white, the Angel Rose appeared in the middle of their circle singing with them. As the men and women on the deck stood in awe of the beautiful Angel she turned her eyes on Admiral Cooper.

"Welcome, James Cooper, you have stood with honor and respect for the children of God when your leaders reviled them. Today, you have given your heart and your life of your own free will, to live for the Son of God. You will be a shining beacon for the service men and women of the armed forces around the world. For the moment, go with the Crossfire Team and they will bring you to a place the Most High has prepared for you where you can join with others to stand against Satan and his Earthly minions."

Rose swirled away and faded from sight.

Mark looked at the Admiral and walked over and hugged the man, "Welcome brother, Did a little praying during the battle?"

Admiral Cooper nodded his head. "Anyone who saw what you and Sarah were fighting against and wouldn't want to have God on their side needs severe mental work." He looked for a minute into Mark's eyes, "Thank you from the bottom of my heart for placing your lives on the line for me."

Mark smiled. "Admiral, you are more than welcome, but, we are merely servants. Give all the praise and glory to God."

The team members remained with the admiral to ensure his safety as he transferred his authority and command to the Captain of the battle cruiser. He said a quick farewell to several people he knew and then got on board the Fragment and left with the team for the Sword.

CHAPTER THIRTEEN

Aboard the Sword, Captain Conners and the XO, Sword Commander Hugh Kelly, greeted Admiral Cooper and accorded him the proper ceremony due a visiting Naval VIP. The Captain and the Admiral had been classmates at the U.S. Naval Academy and were old friends. Actually carrying the rank of Admiral himself, Captain Conners understood the emotions his friend was going through having been suddenly cashiered out of the Navy and being hunted by human and demonic assassins.

The Captain offered the Admiral his command seat on the bridge and gave him the virtual tour of the Sword. "Actually, Jim, the Sword is only another hundred feet longer than the G.W. Bush. The real difference in capacity is the aircraft storage area on the assault deck. They both have three nuclear reactors and good surface speed. The Sword also has full submarine capabilities and can clock over two hundred knots per hour via full cavitation flow. The other advantage is God's Force Generator field which renders this ship indestructible."

Admiral Cooper shook his head, "I've got to see this baby in combat."

Commander Kelly laughed, "Well Sir, the action is extremely violent, even horrific, but in here it's almost boring it's so quiet and calm. The major surprises are announced by an Archangel and the Crossfire Team. Would you like to review several of our recent battles?"

After the Admiral agreed, Kelly showed him multiple views of the destruction of submarines, surface ships, the Rod from Space, and the destruction of the Russian stealth jets with their nuclear missiles. Afterward, the Admiral nodded, "I'm glad that you all are obeying God in these matters, because without that authority, these actions would be criminally illegal and morally reprehensible."

Captain Conners agreed. "But, God is a God of love not hatred or death. These "terminations" were ordered after God gave many chances to the attackers to not to come against God or God's people. In their vanity the attackers ignored God and since our God is also a just God He destroyed them. Yes, we did the destroying. But, if we hadn't done God's will, someone or something else would have. God will not be mocked."

The Admiral asked, "But, I'm sure that all those sailors and pilots didn't personally defy God, why did they have to die just because they were obeying orders?"

"I can't answer that except to say, that they were part of a system that defies God or denies His reality. Individually they will have another chance when they meet God."

The angel Rose appeared suddenly and apologized, "I have need of the Admiral for a short while." Then both the Angel and the Admiral disappeared. Ten minutes later the Angel Hugo appeared with the Admiral. "Sorry about the interruption." Then Hugo disappeared.

Captain Conners looked at the Admiral and raised one eyebrow in question.

The Admiral smiled slightly, "I apologize for being gone for the last three days. It wasn't my idea, but Hugo wanted to give me some training so that I could see the larger picture. It seems that I have been judging everyone else from my own skewed view of Judeo-Christian concepts. You know, I believed that basically everyone is good-hearted, charitable, observes right from wrong, and deep-down inside knows about God. I now have been shown reality. When a person doesn't know about God at all, their "better" nature isn't all that good. Almost every one of the sailors and pilots that were killed attacking you were not generally deserving human beings that were worried about anyone except themselves."

Hugh Kelly smiled, "You tend to get millions of that type of person in atheistic totalitarian regimes,"

Captain Conners nodded, "Don't worry about your absence. Your three-day trip to Heaven translated to roughly ten minutes in our time here on Earth."

The Admiral shook his head. "That is a new concept for me. It'll take me some serious thinking about time to adjust."

Christi asked for permission to enter the bridge and was permitted by Captain Conners. She approached the trio of naval officers. "Pardon my intrusion Captain, General

Malone sent me to bring the Admiral to the team's War Room, there is an emissary there with information on the Admiral's new mission."

The three men made their farewells and Christi led the Admiral back to the team's quarters and the War Room.

As he walked into the futuristic command room the Admiral wasn't surprised to find a different Angel standing near Jack, Mark, Laura, and Sarah. The Angel looked up at the Admiral and smiled at him. Admiral Cooper could have sworn that he could see eons of history in the angel's eyes.

The Angel Caleb was introduced to the Admiral and he had the man sit with the others. "Admiral Cooper, I have been honored to bring the word of the Most High to you. Now hear the Word of the Lord." *"James Cooper, you have truly given your heart and your life of your own free will, to live for the Son of God. God has foreseen this time since before the beginning of this world. There is a cadre of warriors at a dwelling in the city of Jerusalem who are waiting for your leadership to organize and command a force to provide true military guidance for faithful warriors around the world."*

Caleb let the Admiral say his farewells to the Crossfire Team and then they both disappeared.

Mark sat down and asked, "Are we going to interface with the Admiral and his group again?"

Laura, as usual had been praying, looked up and nodded her head, "We are, and in a big way, very soon. I have the impression that one of the ongoing missions for the Crossfire Team will be as assigned by the Father as the defense arm for the Military Source."

Mark grinned, "That's the official name, "The Military Source"?"

Laura nodded. "Also God wants to speak to the entire team tomorrow at six bells of the second watch or seven A.M."

Jack had gotten so accustomed to hearing the bell chimes over the 1MC (communication Center) of the ship he was no longer aware of them happening. Except that he could tell the time without looking at his watch.

After the meeting broke up, Christi came up to Mark and asked, "Would you please explain the bell system to me? Right now I have to look at my watch when I hear them."

Mark nodded, "I've been hearing ships bells for so long it's natural time keeping to me. The day is split into six watches. Each watch is four hours long and the bells are struck thus: Midnight, Morning, Forenoon, Afternoon, Dogs, First.

The bells mark the hours of the watch in half-hour increments. The seamen would know if it were morning, noon, or night. Each bell is thirty minutes long. So, after the first half hour you would have; 1 bell which is 30 minutes, 2 bells at 1 hour, 3 bells at one and a half hours, 4 bells at two hours, 5 bells at two and a half hours, 6 bells at three hours, 7 bells at three and a half hours, and 8 bells is four hours. The end of the watch is considered at 8 bells, hence the saying "Eight Bells and All Is Well". Does that clear it up for you?"

Christi thought about it and said, "Then, six bells of the fourth watch would be three pm for a landlubber?"

Mark grinned, "You got it. Keep at it and in a month you'll instinctively know what time it is by the ship's bell."

CHAPTER FOURTEEN

Jack made certain that the full complement of the Crossfire Team was assembled in the Dining Room/Chow Hall/Conference room the next morning.

Precisely at six bells of the second watch, (0700 hours) Yahveh God's voice sounded throughout the room. *"Warriors of God, I am proud of each and every one of you and the service you have given to the Kingdom in My name and that of My Son. Many of you have forsaken a normal life in the world to serve Me. In the next thirty-four months you will be challenged more than ever before. Some of you will fall and come to live with Me in Heaven during this time. I ask you all to stay the course for your reward will be great in Heaven. There is a powerful new evil arising out of the Far East that threatens all life on Earth, worse than that of Molec! Since your inception, I have trained and positioned your team specifically to war against this threat."*

"If it gets released, everything you know and everything you've learned will be thrown into question when you combat the Chimaera. Stay in prayer and I and my Angels will be with you."

When God ceased talking Jack led everyone in a prayer of thanks to an all-powerful and loving God. Then the questions started.

Mark asked, "What is a Chimera?"

Ethan had already researched the name. "Mark, in Greek mythology a chimera is a fire-breathing female monster with a lion's head, a goat's body, and a serpent's tail. A second and more likely definition is; a thing that is hoped or wished for but in fact, is illusory or impossible to achieve."

Mark snorted, "So our choice is a fire-breathing, female monster lion, goat, snake, or something which is illusory or impossible to achieve? Great choice."

Jack laughed, "I think we need a lot more research."

Christi offered, "If the Lord of the universe thinks it's bad..."

David spoke up, "Actually, I've heard of a Chimera that is a lot more sinister than those two options. As a part of the Mossad I worked a case where a biologically-trained physician created a fiendish new toxic nerve agent he called Chimera."

Mark asked, "what happened?"

David looked very sober, "We were closing in on his lab when he was warned about our raid. He got out with his nerve gas and disappeared. We've been looking for him for the last ten years, nothing."

Christi said, "Oh yeah, I saw a "Mission Impossible" movie about that."

David shook his head, "That was pure imagination, nothing else."

Laura smiled, "Any chance that it is the origin of this evil the Lord mentioned?"

Jack looked at Laura, "The nerve gas or the movie?"

Laura frowned, "The gas, of course."

Jack smiled, "Alright! Everybody start researching Chimera, Use our contacts, and Ethan."

Ethan looked up, "Yes Sir?"

"Start looking in the intelligence files and see if there is any mention of it regardless of the connected reason."

Mark added, "Except if it's about a fire-breathing, female monster lion, goat, snake."

Ethan grinned, "Yes Sirs."

Three hours later Ethan sat down with the Core Team and explained his research findings. He looked around at the expectant faces and sighed. "I have to tell you that my findings are less than happy news. It seems that David is correct in his conjecture that Chimera is a fiendish new toxic nerve agent. It seems this biologically trained physician, named Hermann Grode developed it specifically to destroy all the Jews in Israel. David's Mossad raid ten years ago frightened him so badly he went underground and literally disappeared."

"That is, until this year, when he was spotted by MI-6 at a gambling table in Monaco. He is now an inspector for one of the largest pharmaceutical companies in the world. He actually doesn't have to work because he's worth sixty million U.S. dollars and lives in a villa in southern France. Tracking his funds, it seems he sold an "intellectual property" to an anonymous buyer for fifty million and parlayed the other ten million through an additional second sale, which I doubt the original buyer knows about. The problem we have is the original buyer was the Arab terrorist group, "Mortal Death"."

David scowled, "That is not good for anybody."

Mark shook his head. "Those people are so evil I think our armor and swords would appear if we ran into one. If they bought the poison, they can and will strike anywhere and kill everyone in the area. The only questions are when and how."

Ethan continued, "The reason Grode used the name Chimera is that it represents a single organism composed of genetically distinct cells from different organisms. His toxic nerve agent is a mixture of strains that alter the primary characteristics of the toxin. His toxin is a super killer. It kills the host organism in less than one minute by attacking the blood, turning it into a poison that stops the heart instantly when it enters the heart."

Alexis asked, "How is it transmitted?"

Ethan shook his head, "By direct contact with the skin of the victim. It is not transmitted through the air. The reason for that is that it would kill the people trying to dispense it. People can't be "carriers" of this toxin because it kills so quickly. So, it's not like a plague that wipes out whole countries starting from one person. While it sounds like an advantage in reality it isn't. The multifaceted organism construction allows the terrorists to dispense the toxin through the air but it requires a direct skin contact to affect a person. Not an advantage because if someone walks into a dispersion of the toxin they could breathe it into their lungs without effect because the intracellular transfer destroys the toxin. But if it lands on their person and they try to wipe it off, they are dead."

Mark thought for a bit. "What do the other organism traits do?"

Ethan frowned, "The scientists don't know for sure. But, they are fairly sure that it allows the toxin to remain effective for roughly an hour on all forms of surfaces."

David smacked his fist on the desktop. "Why hasn't this man been arrested and grilled for answers about the toxin and who he sold it to?"

Ethan shook his head, "Because he is being protected by Marco Marino's One-World Government. No one seems to know why."

Laura snorted, "I know why. Because Satan controls all of these characters and he is eager to kill off any and, if possible, all mankind."

Jack was saddened by the total evil of this scheme. "Maybe no one else will touch him but we surely will! David, you and Alexis work out how we can get him for a "discussion" on our terms. Mark you and the rest of the Core Team find out where this Mortal Death group is and let's see if we can destroy the toxin and them. Laura and I are going to pray and see how the Father wants us to approach this."

CHAPTER FIFTEEN

As Jack and his wife prayed for guidance they felt a presence. Looking up they saw the Angel Caleb and four new angels they had not seen before.

Jack smiled, "Shalom, warriors of God! Welcome, have you come in answer to our prayers?"

One of the new angels looked at Jack with some irritation. "Quiet! Mortal, we will discuss this and then tell you what we decide."

Caleb rolled his eyes and frowned over the other angel's stern comments. "Horeb, I suggest you relax and . . ."

Horeb half drew his sword and yelled at Caleb. "I don't need suggestions from you! I am in charge here and I will not be treated so . . ."

Jack had stood up and now stepped between the two angels. Turning to face Horeb he spoke clearly and with force. "You need to leave our presence right now! With your attitude you are not welcome here."

Horeb stared at the human and drawing his sword, he swung a mighty blow at Jack to kill him for his arrogance. When his sword was stopped by the Force Generator field he raised his sword to strike him again when Caleb stepped next to Jack with his sword blocking Horeb's sword.

Jack started praying seeking God's direction and was shocked to see his own armor and sword appear. Jack heard God's voice which said, *"Strike Horeb down, now!"* Jack reached over and easily moved Caleb aside and allowed Horeb to strike him again. As his sword came down it was stopped by the field again. Jack stepped forward and plunged his glowing blade through Horeb's heart in a single massive strike. The Angel staggered and dropped his sword to the floor. He looked up at Jack with eyes full of surprise and disbelief. Then as Jack pulled his sword out, Horeb died and his body collapsed to the floor.

The other three Angels had pulled their swords as if to attack Jack. Caleb stepped next to Jack's right side and Laura stepped up to Jack's left side. The three-to-three standoff lasted for a few seconds before Caleb said, "Everyone sheath their swords, now."

Jack and Laura stopped praying and their armor and swords disappeared. The other Angels put their swords away as did Caleb. He pointed at the other three Angels, "Return, now." They disappeared and the drama level dropped greatly. Caleb bent down and picked up Horeb's body and sword and disappeared without a word.

Laura looked sadly at Jack, "I'm sorry you had to do that, but I too, heard God tell you to strike the Angel down."

Jack nodded, "I didn't want to do that since he couldn't hurt me. But, the Father commanded me to do it. I didn't have a choice. I am afraid that act might have destroyed our friendship with Caleb and possibly all the Angels."

Laura put her arms around Jack and hugged him.

Jack sighed and hugged her back. He was about to go back to praying when Raquel appeared in his Archangel mode. His golden eyes locked with Jack's eyes. He reached out and placed his hand on Jack's shoulder. Peace filled Jack up suddenly, even joy. The Archangel's deep voice filled the room.

"Be at peace Jack Malone, The Most High sent me to ally your concerns in this matter. You're held in esteem by Caleb and the Heavenly Host. Your faith burns brightly and is true. While Caleb is sad about losing an old friend he knew you had no choice. He left before saying anything because he was in shock that a human could kill an Angel. Remember that your armor, sword, Force Generator, and anointing are all from The Most High and would not have worked if the Father had not permitted it."

Jack nodded, "Why would Horeb act like that and then try to kill me?"

"Unfortunately, even Angels are subject to the sin of pride and even though we are spiritual beings we are just as vulnerable as humans are, and pride opens a door through which Satan can slip in and pervert our minds. That's what happened to poor old Horeb."

Jack stared at his friend, "If Angels are spiritual beings how can they die?"

Raquel looked at Jack for a bit, "Like everything in God's Kingdom there are two aspects to Angels also. Let's call one aspect the "here and now" and the other "there and then". While they are serving the Most High they are in the "Here and now". If they are killed in service or in battle, their form remains in the "here and now" but their spiritual essence goes to the "there and then" and is not seen in the "here and now" again. It is not death as you know it but a change in status. That's how I understand it and I don't know any more about it except that they will be reunited with the Most High at some point."

Raquel smiled, "I have to go, someone wants to speak with you."

As the Archangel disappeared, Caleb appeared.

Jack walked over to him and hugged him, "I'm so sorry about your friend."

Caleb put his arms around Jack. "As am I, Jack Malone. But I came back to finish my mission and to tell you and Laura there are no bad feelings concerning Horeb. I was simply amazed that an Angel could be killed by a human, even one as gifted as you are, and I was at a loss for words. I understand now and apologize if my actions caused you concern.

Jack patted the Angel's arm and smiled, "I'm glad you are still our friend. What is the message and while you're here, why did the other four Angels show up?"

Caleb nodded his head, "The reason they came was for familiarization with humans, training they had never received before. I think you opened some eyes. The message was this, Hear the word of the Lord. *"My child, Satan is doing everything he can to make this horror become reality. You and the team must stop it. There is little time before their first strike. The Mortal Death group has penetrated the United States western border and is presently in the city of San Francisco. Talk to Director Jacobson, she will help you find them. Take Raquel, Caleb, and Rose with you."*

Caleb said several words Jack couldn't understand and both the Angel Rose and the Archangel Raquel appeared.

Jack was somewhat at a loss as to what to tell the trio of Angels because he knew that God had made man on Earth lower than the angels, it wasn't until man ascended to heaven that he would judge the angels. Raquel smiled.

"Rest easy Jack, we're here to prevent Satan's troops from interfering with you in this effort."

Jack had really become concerned when he imagined that he would have to command three members of the heavenly host and he blew out a breath and smiled back. "Good, I wasn't sure what "Take the three of you along required." He released that concern from his mind and placed a call to the Mossad Director.

Director Jakobson talked to Jack about the terror group. "Jack, these people are in America in the City of San Francisco to conduct the trial runs with Chimera. They also will announce a list of unreasonable demands to keep them from spreading it farther than the first trial. They don't care if the demands are met or not. They are just adding confusion and false hope which they will then crush."

Jack sighed, "Then we need to crush them before they start. Do you have eyes on them?"

"Loose ones. We have a Kidon team there but they have to keep their distance because there are demons involved. And we've learned our lesson, we can't defeat those things, but they can kill us. We'll wait for your Team to take on the demons.

Jack asked, "Give me an address and we'll be there in three hours or less."

The Director sighed this time. "I've already sent you the address and the Kidon contact. She will wait for your call."

Jack told Iris goodbye and prayed that God would delay the Mortal Death terrorists until they could get there. He called Laura, Mark, Sarah, Carol, Ethan, Elon, and Su Li. He told them, "Full battle gear plus some of the special ammo and grenades to the hanger immediately. Then he called David and Alexis and told them that they were in charge until he returned.

Ten minutes later the away team boarded a "Fragment" and headed for the west coast of America.

Eighty-three minutes later The invisible aircraft settled to the ground in the parking lot in a warehouse district in Daly City southwest of downtown San Francisco.

A lone female was standing near the gate to the deserted parking lot. Jack, Laura, and Elon were dressed in street clothes, left the Fragment, and walked over to where she was standing. Elon greeted her in Hebrew. "Shalom, Ariella, it is good to see you again."

Ariella evaluated the three people and grinned. Shalom, Elon, we've missed you since you moved uptown." She stepped up to him and kissed him on the cheek.

Elon hugged her and turned to introduce Jack and Laura. She greeted them in very good English. "I am honored to meet you both. Your service in the name of Israel has reached the level of legend and I salute all of you and your team.

Laura smiled and gave Ariella a hug. "Thank you Ariella and let us see if we can measure up to our billing this time."

As Jack shook her hand he asked, "Are we still in time to stop their first sortie?"

Ariella nodded her head, "We think so. They are preparing to move out as we speak though. How do you want to handle it?"

"Well, since this is your operation and there isn't time to preplan again, why doesn't your team stop the human part and we'll take care of the demonic as necessary?"

Ariella nodded as she thought to herself, "This was not what I had expected of the Crossfire Team. This could work out very well." She spoke into her cell phone in French to confuse any other listeners. "Chaim, we have the Demon Busters with us. Stop the terrorists and keep the leader Yorik alive, if possible. You know what to do. No explosives! It would release the plague,"

Jack told her, "Give us a minute to get the rest of our crew."

Ariella looked around the large parking lot of several acres of empty parking spaces and said, "How far away are your people? We don't have much time!"

Laura grinned, "Closer than you think, come on."

They walked thirty yards away from the gate and the hatch of the Fragment opened out of thin air. The rest of the Team disembarked as Jack, Laura, and Elon dashed into the plane and quickly put on their battle armor and grabbed their weapons. They exited the hatch, which closed and the Fragment disappeared and silently rose into the sky.

Ariella looked a little irritated, walked over to Jack, felt with her hand, and felt nothing. "Okay, how do you do that?"

Mark smiled, "It is all just smoke and mirrors."

She shook her head, "No, really, how do you do that?"

Sarah took Ariella by the arm and headed her back toward the parking lot gate. It's done by a mixture of faith and technology and if we all live through the next few hours, we'll show you, okay?"

CHAPTER SIXTEEN

Ariella nodded and led the heavily armed team to a position at the end of a huge warehouse. She led Sarah to the corner and pointed out a smaller warehouse about a hundred yards away. "That's where the vermin are hidden. They will be driving out of that rollup door in a few minutes. We are going to stop them just outside the warehouse by disabling their vehicle's engine and release a rapid knockout gas that we've placed in the truck. We then terminate everybody except their leader "Yorik", capture the poison, and get Yorik to confess who gave them the poison."

Sarah looked at Ariella, "That's a great plan, but it won't work."

Ariella looked at Sarah without irritation, "Why won't it work?"

Sarah shook her head, "For the same reason we're here, demons! They will have watched you plant your knockout gas and your remote engine kill switch and told the terrorists about them. It's also possible they listened to your plans and are ready to counter you at every turn."

As Laura listened she started praying that God would aid them in defeating the terrorists and their demons. As she humbled herself the Father dropped a bombshell into her mind. Laura said suddenly, God says this is a trap! There are over forty men in two warehouses armed to the teeth and a bunch of demons. They plan to kill all of us or at least distract us and let Mortal Death escape."

Mark said, "Check your FGs and prepare to stop the hordes. Ariella, you, Laura, and Elon stop Mortal Death and secure the poison. Can you warn your other team mates and get them out of harm's way?"

Ariella knew in her heart that Laura really had heard from God and she nodded. She used her phone and warned Chaim and the others that they had been made and they were to flee, now! She was about to ask what to do when Mark was suddenly covered in brilliant silver armor and held a sword of chrome with waves of energy rolling off of its length.

She stepped back and suddenly realized with a shock that everyone excluding her was covered in gold or silver armor and had those awesome swords. Jack, Laura, and Elon stood around her with their backs to her in a protective circle.

Still shocked by the armor she got a worse shock as two dozen of the most horrible creatures came charging out of a strange rip in the air. These "things" radiated evil and came at the warriors with death in their eyes and something even worse on their minds. Ariella was assaulted by feelings of uselessness, worthlessness, sickness, and every evil and perverted thing that could be done to the human body. She cried out to G-d in her mind for help. A wave of peace came over her. In her relief she realized that Elon had put his hand on her shoulder and all the horrid thoughts were as nothing and had no power over her. He said, "Pray constantly that God will block those curses."

Elon turned back as the first wave of demons reached them.

Ariella was amazed at the viciousness of the demons and their almost mindless attack on the Crossfire Team. But there were gold and silver covered warriors cutting down, up, and sideward through the demons with great efficiency. Sometime they went so fast all she could see were the flashing sword blades. Three of the Team were firing their rifles and killing demons with every shot. Twice they fired grenades, which took out scores of demons. As the number of demons were reduced, Elon and Laura took her by the arms and led her away from the battle and toward the warehouse the terrorists were in.

The rollup door suddenly opened and a black SUV raced out of the warehouse and turned away from the scene of the battle to escape. Laura was talking into her battle communicator and put up a hand to prevent Ariella from chasing after the truck.

Ariella looked at Laura like she'd lost her mind. "Those vermin have the poison!"

Laura only said, "Watch."

Suddenly the truck rose off the ground and shot straight up into the air at an ever-increasing rate of speed unit it became just a dot and then it vanished.

Laura grabbed Ariella and pushed the Israeli woman behind herself and Elon as dozens of bullets were fired in their direction. The bullets hit the two team member's FG fields and dropped to the ground as both Elon and Laura released their swords, which disappeared along with their armor and shields. They brought up their M-8 rifles and returned the fire. The terrorists in the building were relentlessly pouring dozens of rounds at the three people but with no effect. All at once four more rifles were added to the melee as Jack, Mark, Sarah and Christi added their firepower to the battle. Three 40mm grenades devastated the terrorist ranks and the battle was over in less than a minute with no survivors on the terrorist's side.

Jack reported that the demons had been defeated and the rift had closed. Ariella looked at Laura and asked, "All right, what happened to the truck?"

Laura laughed, "Don't worry, they'll be back soon. We can secure the poison they have and interrogate all of them to locate their base and the rest of the poison."

Ariella shook her head, "That's great, but, what happened to the truck and the terrorists?"

Everyone's armor and swords faded out of sight. Laura smiled. "I knew we couldn't catch the truck so I told our aircraft to magnetically lock onto the truck and quickly take it to 35,000 feet altitude. It waited until its sensors registered that the people in the truck were unconscious and is bringing it back right now. They passed out from a lack of oxygen and we should be able to secure them and the Chimera without a problem."

Ariella had been astounded by so many things in the last hour she didn't know if this was normal or not. Resorting to her training she called Chaim and had him and the other two team members come back to the warehouse.

Ariella saw Laura looking up and she looked also. The SUV was coming down to the ground and set down twenty feet in front of the Kidon agent. Both women and Elon advanced on the vehicle with their guns at the ready. They couldn't see anything inside the truck because the windows were frosted over on the inside. Elon tried the driver's door and pulled it open. Inside were four mostly frozen men covered in rime ice with ice on their faces. The other three agents showed up and pried all four of the men out of the truck and onto the ground. They searched the men and bound them. Ariella searched the SUV and found twelve vials of what were most likely the poison and a spraying contraption in the back of the vehicle.

The people from CDC and Homeland Security arrived and took control of the prisoners and the poison. The Crossfire Team and Ariella were gone and, as arranged, Chaim took credit for capturing the terrorists and stopping the biological attack.

CHAPTER SEVENTEEN

Ariella was in a state of overload, sitting in an invisible, hypersonic, and indestructible aircraft following a lead she had found in the SUV. This team was so far advanced in technology and spirituality over the Mossad that she was envious. Not in a mean way but in a "I really wish we had these things" kind of way.

Her thoughts were interrupted as the communications manager, Ethan Reaper, knelt next to her seat and showed her his large tablet display. She looked at the display and was able to see a real-time display of the target building in the Mexican desert outside of San Luis Potosi. The screen showed her three different views of the large ranch-style building. A normal view, a heat signature view, and a detailed floor plan view. The heat view showed eight people in the building at that time. There was a box outside the view with name and specs for each person plus what weapons they were carrying. She looked at the honest face next to her and asked, "Ethan, how can you get all this data and real time views of a place you didn't know about twenty minutes ago?"

Ethan smiled, "This is just a minor effort. The real time views are from a Chinese Spy satellite now over Mexico, the building plans are from the Mexican Tax records, and the heat signatures are from a U. S. Predator drone. These inputs are fed through the Cray computer complex on the Sword and forwarded to this tablet. Of course, none of this is even quasi-legal, but it is extremely helpful."

She shook her head, "What kind of computing power do you need to do this?"

Ethan laughed, "As Rolls Royce says when you ask how much horsepower their engines have. They merely say, "Adequate". "We have a lot more than Adequate computer power."

Jack leaned over and spoke to both Ethan and Ariella, "We're going to be there in six minutes. Get ready to fight. Ariella, that body armor looks good on you."

As the Fragment neared the location Jack had the invisible plane make a close pass to confirm the location.

They were twenty yards from the building when it exploded so violently it knocked down all of the outer buildings and instantly caught them on fire. The center of the blast was so incredibly hot it melted the asphalt driveway 60 feet from the building. As the smoke cloud rose into the daytime sky the fire continued to get hotter instead of cooling down. Sarah and Mark said in unison "Magnesium Fire!".

Ariella was still shaking from the initial explosion that should have vaporized their aircraft. The Force Generator field protecting the Fragment treated the explosion like any other energy. It nullified it completely. The nine people in the Fragment didn't even get jolted by the furiously expanding globe of sheer violence. They were able to sit calmly as the building blew out around them and everything, including the eight people inside the building were reduced to fragments or even molecules.

Jack told the Fragment to head back to their base on the Sword while they attempted to figure out what happened and who caused it and why it was done.

Mark kicked off the discussion with, "Well, we know two things for sure. First, we didn't do it. Second, that blast eliminated any clues as to the remaining poison and anyone there involved in the terrorism. We're back to square one.

Ariella said, "No, we're not. We are fairly certain that everyone in Mortal Death is dead. According to some excellent Intel we know that there were eleven members still alive when they bought the Chimera. I'm fairly certain seven of the eight people we saw on the thermograph, along with the four we caught in San Francisco made up that whole group."

Sarah chimed in at that point. "The only rationale for a Magnesium fire of that size would be so that any supplies of the Chimera in that building would be absolutely destroyed. Could the explosion have been done by people like the CIA or a military group?"

Jack nodded, "Possibly, but we can't be sure of any of the details we've just listed. It's all speculation and that bomb could have as easily set by Mortal Death themselves knowing that there would be no forensic evidence to prove that they weren't killed in there. Plus, we don't know for sure that the poison has really been destroyed."

Laura had been quiet up until then. She stood up and looked around at the group. "I've been praying for insight into this sudden course change in this operation and I can tell you five things that are for sure." That had everyone's attention.

She smiled, "First, seven of the people in that building were the last members of Mortal Death. Second, all of their remaining supplies of Chimera were completely burned up in the fire. Third, this was not just an accidental explosion by clumsy bomb-makers. It was tailor-made to do exactly what it was designed to do. Fourth, it was not set by law enforcement or the military because it was set by a competitor. Fifth, and last, that competitor has a lot more intelligence and assets than the Mortal Death gang has ever had."

Mark frowned, "If it was a competitor why would they destroy the supplies of Chimera instead of keeping them for their own uses?"

Laura looked sad, "Because they already have sufficient quantities to kill everybody in the whole world. Also, the man couldn't go head-to-head with the terrorists, he's not that brave. But, he is smart enough to build a bomb and put it where it would destroy his competition and ensure that there were no samples left for the scientists of the world to develop an anti-toxin from."

Sarah asked," Did you also happen to get a name and location for our bomber?"

Laura shook her head, "No, but I did learn that he is someone we've battled before and he's still under the thumb of Satan."

She looked at Jack, "Remember when we were searching outside of Zyngola for those four MIRVed Russian missiles? We found two and God took care of the other two? Do you remember the person suspected of spiriting them out of Russia and into the hands of the radicals?"

Jack thought for a few seconds. "Oh yeah, some shady character nick-named the "Serpent". Didn't the Mossad tell us that he welched on the men who worked for him and then killed them...with a bomb!"

CHAPTER EIGHTEEN

Mark snapped his fingers, "Dollars to doughnuts he was the second buyer for the Chimera!"

Laura nodded, "I won't take that bet, because I won't get the money and you don't need the doughnuts. Now, how about we all pray to see how the Father wants us to prosecute this character."

Ariella watched as the others, including Elon, stood, sat, or got down on their knees and sang praise songs and worshiped Yahshua and Yahveh. She had seen so many things today that weren't ever discussed at home or in Temple but they had all been wonderful and good things. As a golden and white energy formed among the people praying on how to do God's will she realized that she may not have seen everything yet.

The Angel Rose spun into being and poised floating there in the midst of the warriors as they prayed. She floated to her right and gently put her right hand on Elon's left shoulder. He continued praying but knelt at a better angle than before. While she waited she looked at Ariella and spoke to her in her mind so as to not disturb the prayers. *"Hello Ariella, you look so happy. Be aware the in the very near future all Jews will come to know Yahshua as Savior. So don't be disturbed by the things you see when you're in this company of God's warriors. Know also that both God and His Son truly love you."*

Jack looked up and said, "Welcome beautiful Angel of the Most High Yahveh God. Have you come with a word for us?

All the rest of the Team ceased praying and sat in the seats or on the floor. In her melodic voice the Angel greeted every one and then turned to Elon. "Elon you are quickly becoming a masterful warrior on the field of battle. A word of caution though, instead of trying to block all those black blades with your blade, learn to coordinate the use of your shield with your blade, ask Jack or Hugo to show you how. The shield confuses the normal demon because they can't comprehend the idea of a defensive weapon."

The Angel turned to Jack. She smiled and it lit up the room. "Jack, times have changed since it was only you and Laura against everything, haven't they? I remember when I was worried about how you two and then Mark and Sarah would battle through the enemy. Now I'm confident that your team will total destroy everything of the demonic in a given area. Which I understand from Raquel is Mark's normal plan of combat"

That brought a laugh from everybody. Rose let some of the fierce white power color override the calmer gold. "Now hear the word of the Lord. " *My warriors, the man you seek is named "the Serpent" for good reason. He is deadly to all around him. But, his weakness is his love of mammon. He desires to sell pieces of his cache of death to all the highest bidders. He is going to Amman, Jordan to cull the profit of the earth's oil. I want your Team, along with Ariella to find him, eliminate all of his poison, and then release him. I will mark him as a pariah so all that see him will see him for what he really is. I and my Angels will be with you. Go with my blessings."*

Rose smiled and spun into nothingness. Ariella noticed that the plane's interior became duller without the beautiful Angel.

Jack rose to his feet and looked at the others. "All right, we know who we want and what to do with him. I believe we will continue to have access to our FGs for this effort because we may face some big odds. Elon, Ariella, stick with Sarah and you two keep Ariella safe from harm." He looked around, "Half and half ammo and grenades. Let's change direction toward Amman."

After they were in an amazingly fast transit to Jordan, Ariella asked Elon, "What did Jack mean by "half and half ammo and grenades"?"

Elon smiled at his former teammate, "God has provided the Crossfire Team with special ammunition and other weapons of war that contain a point or core of His righteous power. When this special ammo is used it kills all of the demons that it hits instantly. We use the normal ammo on human targets."

Ariella sat there thoughtful and then asked, "Elon, I get your shift from Judaism to Christianity because what I've seen today has convinced me... No, it has convicted me that Yahshua is, and was the Messiah. But doesn't it hurt when your family and friends disparage you for walking away from the faith of your fathers?"

Elon shook his head, "No, because I know the truth now when my father didn't. Also, I'm still a Jew and observe all the feasts, and Shabbat."

Ariella sadly looked at her friend, "How can you be sure you're doing the right thing?"

Elon smiled, "Because I've met and talked with Yahshua alone and in a group, several times. He is the righteous Son of Almighty God and awesome beyond belief!"

Ariella looked doubtful, "Really?"

Elon stared at her for a few seconds. "Raquel."

The Archangel appeared next to Elon's seat. "Yes Elon?"

Elon smiled again. "Mighty Angel, would you give Ariella your tour of Heaven so that she'll understand the truth of Yahshua?"

Raquel, Ariella, and Elon disappeared only to return less than a minute later. Both humans thanked the Archangel with tears in their eyes. Raquel winked at Laura and Jack and disappeared again.

Elon was quietly reviewing in his mind all that they experienced in three days in Heaven. Ariella's face had a glow to it as she smiled at the other teammates.

Seeing the glow, Laura elbowed Jack in the ribs, "She got to meet the Savior." Jack just smiled and nodded.

Laura got up, went over, and asked Ariella how she found her time with Raquel.

Ariella smiled and said, "Not to belabor the obvious, I found everything Heavenly. I didn't want to come back but, Yahshua asked me to fight for Him for a while longer and I said "yes", like I could ever refuse him."

Laura thought for a few seconds. She reached over and pushed the green switch on the body armor Ariella was wearing. The LED came on a solid green. Laura smiled, "And you gave your heart to him too."

Ariella looked solidly into Laura's eyes, "YES! I gave my heart and my life to Him and He now lives in me."

Laura leaned down and hugged the Israeli woman, "Welcome Sister".

Elon looked at his former Kidon teammate and shook his head. "You know; you've just ruined yourself for the Kidon for now. You might as well join us and help kill demons."

Laura called Jack, Mark, and Sarah over to the little group. Explaining Ariella's change in status she pointed out the indicator on Ariella's armor. "Think we should offer to steal another one of the Kidon's brightest and best for the Team?"

Jack got approvals from Mark and Sarah and he agreed. "God is never wrong about who He calls into service with us."

He looked at Ariella, "Are willing to change groups and make a lot more money in the service of Yahveh and Yahshua?"

Ariella nodded, "Yes I am."

Laura said, "That was quick. You didn't even stop to think about what it will mean to you,"

Ariella laughed, "This is exactly what Yahshua said you'd ask me. I've thought about everything since then. That was two days ago in my time, remember? And I told Him then that I would say yes. I just had to wait for you guys to ask me."

Jack grinned, "Welcome to the Team. We'll do the paperwork when we get back." He stepped away and spoke to Ethan. "Add Ariella Goldman to the Team's roster as of now and we will give you the particulars when we return to the Sword."

Elon reached over and took Ariella's hand, "Hi again, teammate. You can turn off your Field Generator until we're ready to go into battle. Also, I doubt that the Kidon management is going to see, first me and now you, changing groups as a healthy trend for their agency."

She smiled, switched off the FG switch, "Then they need to take that problem up with God."

CHAPTER NINETEEN

As the Fragment invisibly approached Amman, Jordan; Jack watched the targeting ring on the screen in his combat reticule zero in on a single room in an expensive hotel. Ethan had caught a break from a Mossad, in-place agent who recognized the Serpent from a previous photo and called the info into his superiors. Knowing the Serpent's recent association with demonic bad guys, they called the Crossfire Team. Ethan had intercepted the call and dropped it onto Jack's battle comm.

The deep thermal scan of the suite of rooms by the Ghost showed two people in the bedroom. Jack picked Mark, Sarah, and Ariella to confront the target while the rest of the team worked to contain the situation.

Mark was about to use det-cord to gain entry without going through the lobby when Raquel appeared and suddenly the three of them and the Archangel were in the main room of the suite. Mark nodded to Raquel who vanished. Knowing that Ethan was watching the thermal scan and would notify them of any changes, Mark and Sarah quietly breached the bedroom and caught the Serpent with his lady friend cold. Two stun guns put both the man and the woman to sleep without having any idea they'd be discovered. Two injections later, the three Team members slid the Serpent into a body bag and moved him to the floor of the main room. Mark looked up, "Raquel, four to beam up."

They found themselves back in the Ghost with the Serpent in the body bag. Mark said, "Thank you."

Jack ran a DNA kit against a sample the Mossad had and it confirmed it was the Serpent. Jack had the Fragment return them to the Sword, their ship-based headquarters.

An hour after their return the Serpent regained conscience and found himself securely bound to a hard chair in a small cell. He waited quietly until Mark entered the cell and sat down in front of him. Then, with complete disregard for his situation he asked, "What do you want?"

Mark studied the man for a few minutes before answering. "I want you to tell me where all the amounts of the poison called Chimera that you have, are located."

The Serpent looked quietly at Mark. "Why should I tell you anything? You haven't offered me anything in return."

Mark asked, "What do you want?"

The Serpent smiled, "I want to be free again and retain my wealth."

Mark nodded, "Done." As soon as we have eliminated this poison from the world, we will release you without harm and you can continue to keep your fortunes. But! If you try to mislead us, or cheat in any way on our agreement, your life is forfeit and your fortune becomes our property, even your most secret accounts like the one in the Bahamas."

FaqAbdullah, aka the "Serpent", realized these people knew more about him than he thought humanly possible.

He nodded, "Agreed."

Mark sat there and waited.

The Serpent said, "You realize the enormous funds you're throwing away by not selling this last remaining amount of Chimera?"

Mark didn't flinch, "The location of the remnants of the poison?"

The Serpent sighed, "The entire remnant of the Chimera is in a locked vault in the city of Paris, France. The bank is QMP Paribas and the account number and access code are as follows." After giving Mark the information, the Serpent said, "I would be extremely careful in handling the contents of that vault."

Mark prayed silently, "Father Yahveh, in the name of Yahshua is this man telling the truth about this poison? Is this everything he knows about it and is this truly, ALL that he possesses?"

Mark heard clearly, "No, he has a secret amount in a refrigerated storage unit under a house in Madrid, Spain. It is located at 26929 Villanueva del Pardillo. That is everything he has."

Mark looked at the man. "Are you sure this is all of the Chimera you have? This is your last chance to tell me."

The Serpent sighed, "I give you my word that is all the Chimera I have."

Mark shook his head. "Sadly, you are lying. The terms of this agreement are broken and you will now face judgment."

The Serpent laughed, "You were never going to release me at all! This was just a charade!"

Mark stared at the man, "You didn't reveal the amount stored at Villanueva del Pardillo. That is what prevents me from freeing you. Unless ..."

Realizing he was completely out of options he grabbed at a possible straw. "Unless, what?"

You give me a signed statement of how you were able to buy the Chimera from Hermann Grode."

Henry Fontaine didn't give a hoot about anyone else but himself. He'd gladly give up Grode to save his life. "I will do that. And if I do, you promise you will set me free and I can keep the monies I've earned?"

Mark agreed.

The Team returned to the Sword with their mission accomplished and a new teammate.

The Chimera was recovered by experts from both of the Serpent's vaults and totally destroyed before any military/political organization decided to keep some for "research". They took the Serpent to his villa in Madrid. He laughed to himself at their stupidity for releasing him.

Hermann Grode was arrested and found guilty of crimes against humanity (aka terrorism) and put to death in a prison in Italy.

The Serpent found himself so despised and hated by everyone wherever he went, he lost his fortunes and eventually committed suicide.

CHAPTER TWENTY

In the United States, in the State of Colorado, a young girl had finally reached her limit and yelled at God.

Zoe Lawson told God that wanted to scream, and cry her eyes out, and hurt something very badly and just give up! It absolutely wasn't fair!

She was only seventeen after all and this should not be her life. She missed her Mom and Dad every minute of every day and she had no one to guide her, or help her. Worse yet, she couldn't do any of the things she felt like because the children would see and it would frighten them terribly. They depended on her to be their source of calm reason and it was important that she was there for them.

Zoe looked at the five little kids, two girls and three boys all under the age of four years old. They bravely kept up with her when they had to move and tried in their childish ways to help her. The sad part, which the kids were unaware of so far, was that they were running out of everything at the same time, food, clean water, clean clothes, diapers, and heat. Zoe thought back to when this phase of her life started.

-------------------------*****-------------------------

After her parents disappeared three years ago she had been placed in a camp where there were hundreds of adults and a few very young babies or toddlers. As far as she could tell there were almost no other teens like her. She was befriended by a young couple and stayed with them for almost a year and a half. That was where she had come to understand what happened to her parents and a lot of her friends. Trey, the young man told her about Jesus, God, and the Rapture. It dawned on her that her mother had been right about church. She knew that as a teen she was rebellious and didn't pay any attention to the singing and prayers and the message of the gospel. She thought she had known better than her parents. Now she knew they had been called to heaven to live with Jesus and she hadn't.

In the nights on her cot she started seeking Jesus and prayed the way Trey had taught her. She felt in her heart she wanted to belong to Him. She knew it was a little late, but that stubbornness that she was sure had made her miss the Rapture drove her just as hard to be a believer. She read the Bible every day because she had become fascinated with the stories and one day during her prayers Jesus came into her heart and told her He loved her forever, and she gave her heart to Him without reservation. She sat and listened to Trey and his wife, Heather, as they told her about ways to be a true follower which would please both Jesus and His Father, God. They instilled in her God's love and His desire that everyone would love each other and do good deeds to those needier than themselves.

They warned her that the people who ran the camp were not Christians but followed the Anti-Christ, a man named Marco Marino who didn't like Jesus. They also warned her that if they tried to give her a "mark" or put something under her skin it would separate her from Jesus and His Father forever.

It was less than a month later when the announcement was made over the loudspeakers that everyone in the camp would have an identity chip provided to them for free. It was also mandatory for everyone without exception.

She told Trey she didn't want to take it. He agreed and whispered to her that He and Heather were going to sneak out of the camp that night. She decided to go with them. They had saved a lot of their meals and were taking them with them for food after they escaped the camp.

During that day she tried to act normal and do what she did every other day so that the guards wouldn't suspect anything.

Zoe was nervous about trying to sneak out of the camp for fear they be caught and she prayed for peace and protection for all three of them. She did get peace and was sure her decision to leave was the right one after she heard what the camp directors were going to do to those who refused the chip. They had erected a large machine with a heavy blade and they would use that thing to cut those people's heads off!

CHAPTER TWENTY-ONE

Trey got Zoe's attention around one o'clock the next morning. She was already dressed and snuck quietly along with Trey and Heather through the dark and quiet camp until they reached the fence on the back side of the camp. Someone had cut out a big section of the fence and they quickly ran through the hole and into the trees.

They headed West away from the camp for several hours and it was exhilarating to be free. Just after dawn Trey got frantic and hustled the three of them off the trail they were on and into a cave. Zoe could hear the sound of motors way off behind them, but they were getting closer very quickly.

As they moved far back into the cave they found a whole bunch of people from the camp there ahead of them. Everyone was sitting quietly so that the people behind them wouldn't find them. Eventually the trucks or whatever had passed the cave and the sound disappeared.

Zoe waited with everyone until there was a big discussion and the people start getting up and moving out of the cave into the sunny afternoon.

Terry came back and told her, "Zoe, we need for you to stay here and watch a few of the younger kids while we scout out the area and make sure the camp people aren't around here anymore. Stay as quiet as possible so that no one will find you, okay?"

Zoe wanted to go but agreed to watch the kids for a little while. Eventually, everyone except her and five young children left. She played quietly with the kids until she got bored. Then she went further back in the cave with the flashlight to explore.

Needless to say, the little kids followed her because she was nice and she had the only light. She went around two bends and found a cute little sub-cave where everyone had left their food and baggage while they were scouting.

She was about to go back when she heard loud voices in the front of the cave. She told the kids to sit down and be quiet. Then she turned out the flashlight. She reached out in the dark and touched each of the five children to reassure them that she was still there. There was a lot of loud talking and flashes of lights. Eventually, it got quiet and dark again.

As she waited, she prayed quietly that Jesus would tell her what to do. She was afraid that the camp people had captured Terry, Heather, and all the other adults and nobody was going to come back. Now she was on her own again but she had five little kids to take care of as well as herself. She didn't want to let them down or get them hurt in any way. As the people in the main part of the cave left, she cried out in her mind to Jesus to help her save the children.

She felt a peace come over her and ideas on what to do. No direct words or verses, just ideas. She prayed her thanks to God and turned on the flashlight.

After ensuring that there weren't any guards around outside the cave she took the kids back into the small sub-cave and packed up all the food and supplies and water she could carry in one of the backpacks that had been left behind. She knelt down and told the kids that they were going camping and they had to be as quiet as possible.

Zoe led the kids out of the cave and went the opposite direction from the way they had come to the cave. The way she picked was uphill and harder but safer.

It took her most of an hour before they reached the top of the of the hill and she took off the backpack and set it down. She had the kids sit down while she went up to the top of the hill and looked over. She immediately dropped to her hands and knees and stayed low to remain unseen from the people below.

She had to wipe the tears away from her eyes and keep from screaming. She saw the trucks from the camp and watched as the guards loaded the bodies of the people she had been with in the cave last night. She cried even more when she saw one of the bodies had on the blouse that Heather had worn last night. She slid down from the crest of the hilltop and hurried back to the children. She put on a happy face and the backpack and led the kids away from the hilltop and over several more hills to the south and away from the guards.

Zoe knew better than to go near any place that was inhabited or travel anything like roads or waterways. So she kept their distance from towns or houses. They moved constantly southward in the foothills and ate sparingly from their supplies and water. When the sun was on the tops of the mountains to the west they would find a place that was level and hidden from the lowlands. They would put up their one tent and the bedding they had and then make a fire and eat supper. As it got dark they would clean their dishes and take care of potty breaks. Then they'd lay down, cover up, and go to sleep.

The next morning it was up with the sun, clean up to hide the camp. Once she was sure they had erased all traces, they would head south again.

On the eighth day they woke to a downpour and had to spend all day in the tent because of the heavy rainfall. The next two days they had to slog through wet grass and shrubbery.

The extra effort took a toll on the kids and it required more food and extra breaks to keep moving at all. Zoe was concerned that they were running out of everything with no prospects for new supplies.

-------------------------*****-------------------------

Zoe came back to the present and reassured the kids that everything would be okay. Little Michael had a cough that was getting worse and she didn't have any more medicine to help him. Mary and Tiffany were quiet but well physically. Ben was simply a future Marine. Nothing fazed him and Zoe was pretty sure that any disease like a cold was afraid to attach itself to Ben. He was only four years old and already a force to be reckoned with. Last, but not least, was Rachel. She was also quiet and very observant. Zoe liked that as young as Rachel was, she was always helping her and the other kids.

Zoe had had to carry Michael most of the day because he had pretty well run out of energy. She put him down and covered him with their one, thin little blanket. Then she sat down to rest and prayed that Jesus would protect them and provide for them. She was looking out over a large open field when she noticed someone coming toward them through the high corn in the field. She wanted to get the kids away but the person was almost upon them already.

Zoe stood up and told the kids to move back and run away when they could. She was sure this person would take her into custody.

The last row of corn was brushed aside and Zoe almost fainted from fear. The kids were whimpering, crying, and apparently frozen in place. The "person" was horribly deformed and ugly. He had cold red eyes, sharp black teeth, and a black sword in his hand. He was drooling and grunting as he stalked toward the little group.

Although the evil he was emitting was terrifying and scared her so bad, Zoe knew she couldn't let him get to the little kids. She made her feet move and put herself between the onrushing horror and the kids. She said a quick and fervent prayer to Jesus to let her keep the "man" busy while the little ones could run away and hide.

The man grinned an evil grin and stomped toward her with death in his eyes. He raised the black sword and just when Zoe knew she was about to die, she heard a lovely voice from behind the man say, "Hey jerk-face, I've got a bone to pick with you!"

The "man" spun around and beyond his blotchy skin Zoe saw a beautiful young woman with blonde hair and blue eyes standing there with one hand on her hip. Zoe cried out to Jesus in her mind and asked Him to save this brave woman. Zoe was now so scared she was shaking with fear.

The evil man raised his sword and charged the woman while screaming something horrible. The woman suddenly changed into a golden figure with a glowing sword who cut the man down in three strikes. Then the strangest thing happened. The man turned into a sort of smoke and disappeared. Zoe suddenly collapsed onto the ground with no strength to stop herself. She watched as the woman's armor and sword faded out of sight and then the woman ran over to her.

The woman knelt down and checked Zoe's pulse and then raised her feet up and put the backpack under her feet. She opened one of the girl's eyes and grinned at her. "You're going to be okay. Just rest there for a little bit."

Zoe watched the woman as she touched the belt she wore and listened to her discussion with somebody called "Ethan". Zoe then saw the pistol in a holster on her belt. "Ethan, Christi. I found her and the kids. We're about twenty-six miles away from her last reported position. They are all okay but it was a near thing. The people that run the camp she was in couldn't find them, so they sent a demon to finish them off. Yeah, A teenage girl and five little children. Those followers of Marco Marino have no love or decency. This girl, the kids call her Zoe, doesn't even have as much as a pocketknife and yet she deliberately put herself in front of the demon to keep the kids safe. For a girl just barely out of childhood herself, who probably hasn't ever seen a demon before, that's just gutsy. Listen Ethan, I get the impression these kids have been living in the wild since the adults were ambushed. They need some medical attention and food plus a safe place to recover right now. What have we got in the area?" She listened for several seconds and then responded, "Okay, we'll be ready."

Zoe put her feet down on the ground and sat up. She was feeling better and wanted to help not just lay around. She got to her feet and approached Christi. "Is there anything I can do to help?

Christi was hugging Ben and smiling at the other kids who looked at her in awe after what she did to the mean man. She looked at Zoe with some concern. "Are you alright? My name is Christi and I'm sorry I couldn't get here before that thing found you." Christi then smiled at her and told her, "Zoë, that was a brave thing you did for the kids and Jesus loves you for being willing to put yourself in harm's way for those less capable than yourself."

Zoe felt relief when she heard the name of Jesus. "Are you an Angel, Christi?"

Christi tousled Ben's hair and laughed, "No, I'm not an Angel, but I know several of them."

Zoe blinked several times. "But, how did you know that demon was after us? And where we were, and where did that golden armor and sword come from?"

Christi smiled at the young girl. "The group I'm belong to is called the Crossfire Team; and God has anointed us to battle things like the one you saw. We are followers of

Jesus and we do His bidding here on Earth. He told us that you were in peril and dispatched us to find you and protect you. Your prayers are powerful and God heard you in Heaven. That was what brought us into your lives. Now, get anything you really want to keep and get ready for a special plane ride. We are going to where you'll all be safe." The kids all danced around and yelled in happiness.

CHAPTER TWENTY-TWO

One of the Team's UAVs, a small one, called a "Fragment", landed a hundred feet away from the group and opened its portal. Christi got Zoe and all five kids into the aircraft and belted them into seats. Rachel looked up and asked, "What was that tingly feeling I felt when we got on?"

Christi kneeled down so she was more on Rachel's level. "That, my dear, is the power of God that protects this plane. Nothing can hurt you while you're in His protection."

Rachel smiled, "I love God".

Christi nodded, "Me too."

Ten minutes later the Fragment landed on the Sword and was drawn into the hull. When the portal lifted, Laura and Alexis were waiting and helped Christi and Zoe take the kids up to the medical center for a checkup.

Later that day, after Zoe and the kids had a hot meal and got to sleep for a while in real beds, Christi got one of the women of the SOG to take the kids down to the small park-like area they had in section T of the Sword. There the kids could play for the first time in weeks and have ice cream cones and watch cartoons on a really big screen.

Christi and Zoe sat down in the living area with Laura and Jack and listened to Zoe's tale about her life and especially the time since they left the camp. Laura suggested that they pray and see what The father or His Son wanted Zoe and the kids to do.

It was a simple prayer but it had unusual results.

Raquel appeared sitting next to Laura. Zoe's eyes were big as she looked at Raquel. Christi looked at Zoe," Now, He IS an Angel!"

Raquel smiled at Zoe and nodded." Hi Zoe, I bring you greetings from Jesus and Father God. You are very special to them."

Zoe was enthralled with Raquel and his message. "Hi" was all she could say.

Raquel turned his golden eyes to Jack. "The Most High has a secure place for the five children with Trey and Heather Ross."

Zoe was startled, "Did they live through the ambush?"

Raquel smiled, "Yes they did. We protected them and took them to a safe place that was several hundred miles away from the camp you all were in. This place is in the State of Texas, which doesn't agree with the Anti-Christ and his control. People are still free there for the most part. That is where the little children will grow up."

Zoe smiled, "I'm glad for their sakes because Trey and Heather will love them and take good care of them." She sighed, "What about me?"

Raquel smiled at Zoe. "You have a calling on your life that the Most High gave you before you were born. Because of your Mother and Father's faith in Jesus you would have gone with your parents in the calling up of the saints but God in Heaven wants your help here on Earth for a while longer."

Just then Carol Moffet walked over to the group. Jack introduced Carol to Zoe and asked Carol what she needed.

Carol smiled, "I need my assistant-to-be. Hugo wants to meet her and talk to her."

Jack was somewhat confused. "assistant-to-be? Carol, you need to talk to me. I don't think that I've heard about this.

Equally confused, Zoe said, what is an assistant-to-be? To who? For what?

Raquel laughed. "Carol was referring to you, Zoe."

Zoe looked startled, "Me? I don't even know what Carol does; so how can I be her assistant?"

Raquel nodded, "That's true, right now. But if you'll look into your heart you'll find that is your calling although you will not be an office assistant. Yours is a higher calling. You're going to become God's assistant to your Watcher on the Wallin the supernatural arena. A calling that you are uniquely capable of doing."

Jack chuckled, "Well, as usual, God has everything going the way He wants it to go." He looked at Carol. "Give Zoe some time to say goodbye to the kids and talk to Laura and Christi about the Team, Yahshua, faith and love."

Zoe turned to Christi, "Is this really true?" She looked at Raquel "Is my future to be working for Jesus and Father God?"

Christi smiled and nodded to the Archangel. Raquel stood up and held out his hand to Zoe. "Come, Zoe Lawson, let me show you and the children where I live. Zoe grinned and jumped up and took his hand. They disappeared leaving a great wave of peace in their place.

CHAPTER TWENTY-THREE

Life on the Sword got back to normal for everyone. Battles were few and small as the Anti-Christ and Satan attended to not only more pressing issues but also, one where battles could be won.

In this peaceful and restful time Raquel appeared to the assembled Core Team. His golden eyes locked onto Mark, "The Most High has a mission for the members of this Team that has extremely critical importance in the Heavenlies. It is along the lines of the road trip to hell and the trip to Siberia that never happened. God needs you to correct a situation that should never have happened and one that has resulted from a prior action by the Crossfire Team."

Mark nodded his head, "The Most High knows we will accept any task or mission He gives us. What is the task?"

The Archangel sat down in the air and smiled.

"At the time God ended the time-line of the nuclear-powered invasion of demons in Siberia it ended the life of one of the two associates reading the occult book to open the rift in the Russian laboratory in Siberia. When Sarah threw the bomb at the pentagram below her, she killed all three men. When God ended that time line and started a new one from the time before the invasion it was exactly the same but it was if those three never existed."

Raquel smiled, "Now the problem is that the man, Serge, was also an important factor in the Russian underground. Not the criminal one, the anti-social one. He had influenced his longtime girlfriend, Svetlana Datsishin, to help disillusion the common people about the current Russian government's policies regarding nuclear weapons. Now, in this time, he hasn't existed and she's about to introduce a new line of dresses to the people instead."

Raquel looked at Mark. "Doesn't sound like a problem, especially your kind of problem, right?"

Mark nodded, "That is pretty much what I was thinking."

The Archangel smiled, "Add this into your understanding. In the previous timeline, Svetlana had been coached and trained to walk into the annual meeting of Russian nuclear scientists two days ago and detonate a small, briefcase nuclear weapon that would set back Russian nuclear technology by five years. That would allow America and Israeli scientists to develop a truly fail-safe defense against Russian nuclear missiles."

Raquel looked at the assembled warriors. "But since he doesn't exist, she will not blow up the Russian scientists and Russia will develop a new missile defense system in the next month that will allow them to threaten the Anti-Christ with total destruction of America and Europe as well as the Middle East" without fear of retaliation. This goes against Biblical prophecy and will delay the return of Yahshua to the Earth by decades."

Laura spoke up. "But God will not allow that to happen, will He? He can prevent Russia from developing the new defense system, right?"

The Archangel nodded his head. "Yes He can, and this mission is designed to do exactly that. He is depending on you fourteen people to prevent Russia from creating this new defense system."

Jack thought you could have heard a pin drop to the floor it was so quiet in the War Room. "Why did He pick us?"

"Because the whole concept is based on bad data covered and amended by demonic manipulation to make it "seem" to work."

Mark slapped his hand on his desk. "That way the devil gets Russia to attack the free world killing most of the population. Then, they themselves will be wiped out by a massive retaliation from dozens of nuclear countries that the Russians believe their new system will save them from! World annihilation underwritten by Satan!

Alexis spoke up, "And we are the only Team that can battle the demons in charge of maintaining the illusion that the new system works, right"?

Sarah added "And, demons who will take our intrusion as cause for an all-out attack on us."

Raquel nodded, "Now you begin to see the problem and the answer to "Why us?" but, there is more."

Christi sat back and smiled, "Now for the "other shoe" right, Raquel?"

The Archangel sighed, "Yes, Christi, now for the hard part."

Everyone waited expectantly as Raquel slowly looked at each one of the Core Team.

The Archangel focused on Jack. "Because to accomplish this mission your involvement must be completely unknown by Russian scientists or their government charged with developing the new defense. The Crossfire Team is now universally hated by Russians everywhere because of your multiple defeats of their attempts to kill you." If they find out who you really are they will ignore everything and, goaded by the demons, they will accelerate toward world annihilation. You need to find a way that shows the system's inability to stop foreign missiles without leaving any traces that you were involved."

Mark asked, "We are super easy for the demons to identify if we could even get by the facial recognition systems and the Russian police and military FSB for who a top priority is detection and elimination of the Crossfire Team."

Jack shook his head. "Why not just have the Angels do the mission?"

"Because we are not creative like you are and the Most High believes your team's "take" on things will be crucial to convincing the powers in Russia that their new shield technology doesn't work."

Mark thought for several minutes. "Then I think we need one more operative to help us."

Laura was about to ask who Mark wanted when her Comm unit beeped. She answered and heard the loud, gruff tones of ex-Russian General Demetri Serakov who had defected from Russia and was now employed in helping train the U.S. military.

"Laura! Hello. I am glad to hear from you again. I am outside your part of this marvelous ship. Can you come and let me in?"

She smiled, "Sure thing Demetri, give us a minute."

She looked at Mark, "Your additional mission person stands at the door, waiting."

Mark smiled, "Thank you, Father God."

He jumped up and went to the portal. When it opened he said, "Hi Demitri".

The big bear of a man looked at Mark, "You called?"

After handshakes and hugs the two men returned to the War Room.

Raquel smiled at Demitri. "Would you like me to explain the mission for you?"

Demitri laughed, "No need to do that. It is crisis, the world will end if we fail, we have to do something to Russia, it's dangerous and we may not survive the mission. With this group, this is normal operation. Whatever it is, I'm agreeing with it. What do we have to do first? Or is it a Mark Connelly Op where we go in, kill everybody and leave?"

The Archangel shook his head, "The first thing you need to do is to penetrate Project 5008,somehow,to expose the falseness of their results while avoiding conflict with the demons and their effort to destroy the entire population of the world through nuclear conflict and who don't see failure as an option."

CHAPTER TWENTY-FOUR

Demitri sat up straight, "That is the most secret group in Russia! Nobody is supposed to even know this group even exists, let alone penetrate it! How do you know about Project 5008?"

Raquel used his thumb to indicate himself, "Angel, remember?"

"OH, Da!" Demitri was embarrassed that he had forgotten that fact. "I don't even know what the security is for that group. They don't have any connection to the rest of Russia, Not even internet. It is probably the most secure site in Russia. Nobody gets in other than the scientists and their security, ever."

Ethan Reaper nodded in agreement and joined in, "The black hole they work in only uses an ultra-secure intranet within their group, there is no internet connection for us to sneak into their communications unless we can get inside the actual building they are in. Wherever that is located."

Jack looked at the Archangel, "How much time do we have to find them, penetrate the project, and discredit the missile defense system?"

"They've scheduled the final test for next week. Starting tomorrow you will have less than twelve days. If the last test is declared a complete success, then the government will have a green light to demand capitulation from Marco Marino who won't agree, an action which leads to the final conflict.

Mark nodded his head, "That should be enough time to throw a monkey wrench into the works.

Demitri looked at Mark, "This really is the end of the world, for everyone."

Jack smiled at the downcast ex-Russian. "Not if we can help it and not on my watch!"

Christi asked Raquel, "Why can't God simply have the last test fail?"

Raquel looked at her for several seconds before answering. "Because Satan is using previous agreements or commitments that the Most High made long ago that would require Him to break His own word, which He will not do."

The Archangel rose in the air and looked at everyone in the War Room. He empathized his next words and you could tell there was real passion behind them. "Don't you all see? God can do anything, but to break his word even to prevent the loss of all life on Earth would lead to utter chaos and end all life on Earth anyway. Because if He wasn't true then no one else would be in sin for lying which would quickly lead to the end of truth. Then He would be wrong to deny liars a right to heaven, which He won't do. Then the end of mankind is assured! He is depending on you to solve this problem!"

Jack looked at the faces around him and could see the determination to live up to God's expectations. He stood up and addressed the Archangel. "We will make it happen."

Raquel smiled slightly, and said as he faded out of sight, "Yes, I know you will."

Mark stood up, "Everyone, use your best means that are undetectable and let's find out everything we can about this Project 5008. If anyone, or anything detects us researching this project we might as well just tell the Russians we're involved. Now, I want to have a workable plan in 24 hours. Move it, the clock is running!"

Ethan, along with Charlie and Linda Wu went to the ComSec area to use the computers to search for information. Supported by Ethan, Charlie dared another penetration of the Chinese databases while his wife did the same with the American CIA and British MI-6 files.

David Zahavy worked the Mossad and IDF files. Alexis took Christi with her as she broke into the files of her old employer, The National Clandestine Service in Washington D.C.

Carol spent her time at the timelines interpreting the Matrix for any plans or assignments concerning Project 5008 and working with the Angel Hugo.

At three a.m. Mark called a Core Team meeting to discuss any progress.

Alexis and Christi started off with their discoveries. "The National Clandestine Service has determined that Project 5008 has a mandatory minimum of two weeks to one month to vet any new members allowed to join the project, no exceptions."

David and Sarah had tapped the files of the Mossad on Project 5008. "They have no more than a name for this effort."

Ethan summarized his and the Wu's findings. "China is very aware of Project 5008 and have some inside source of information which has just advised them that the project's final test has been moved up to two days from now and the project has been "sealed" until after the test."

Mark grimaced, "The demons have probably found out we are involved. That would explain the hurry-up date and the sealing of the project to prevent our interference."

Mark was becoming frustrated with the lack of a clear plan to debunk the tests. "All right, we still have the same requirements and now we only 48 hours. Has anybody got an answer?

Christi stood up, "I don't have a plan but I do have a concept that would take all our efforts and could still achieve our goal within the time limit."

Mark stared at her and thought back over her successes so far and it gave him hope. He waved his hand at said, "Christi, you have the floor and I can assure you we are all ears."

After Christi presented her concept it was eagerly accepted by the Core Team and they hurriedly set to work to make it a reality.

By the time they were finished there was only one hour to the test time. That time flew by and reached its end. Ethan announced that the test missile had not been stopped and there had been an explosion at the target site. The Core Team broke out into cheers and applause.

Raquel appeared smiling. "Incredible! None of you even left the ship but you made the test a complete failure. The Heavenly Host gives you all our Congratulations." He disappeared.

Jack congratulated the crew and personally thanked Christi for her ideas. Mark added, "Christi, you've got my share of the bonus for this mission young lady. That sentiment was echoed by Sarah and suddenly everyone on the Core Team did likewise, David laughed, "You more than deserve it all Christi, that idea saved the team and probably the entire human race too this time."

Christi stood up and thanked everyone. "I must refuse all your offers as much as I appreciate your generosity. True, I had the idea but it took all of our combined efforts to make it work. We are a team, in the service of our God that is the way we roll."

CHAPTER TWENTY-FIVE

The Team broke up and headed to their apartments to get some well-deserved rest. Before Jack and Laura left, they prayed, expressing the team's thanks to Yahveh and the success of the mission.

Jack's personal cell phone chirped and he recognized the caller. "Hello Iris, how can we help you?"

The Director of the Mossad was obviously excited and her eagerness was evident in her voice. "Okay Jack, how did you do it? Don't say you didn't make the Russian test of Department 5008 fail! I've seen enough of the Crossfire Team's operations to know its signature when I see it. Plus, G-d said you did it. How?"

Jack grinned, "I will tell you and only you that we were behind the failure. Our second newest member, Christi Steele came up with a last-minute plan that pulled us out of failing to meet Yahveh's command to prevent the final test of the new Russian Missile Shield from seeming to succeed. I had to call in several favors from an old Chinese friend, Zhou Tangtao."

Iris interrupted. "The Vice Premier of China? He's an old friend of yours?"

Jack chuckled, "Iris, don't tell me your organization doesn't know all about our little trip to China a year or so back."

She laughed back, "Well, maybe a little."

Jack resumed his tale. "I explained God's mission and the demonic involvement as well as what God said would be the actual results if the demonically controlled "successful" outcome actually occurred. Then I asked him to pray about our plan and seek the Father's concurrence to help us prevent Satan from faking a successful test. He agreed and called me back in minutes. He said the Lord wanted him to help us."

"Now understand that none of this should ever be spoken of or written about until Zhou leaves his position in the Chinese government. Please, for everyone's sake, delete the recording you're making of this call."

Iris agreed and stopped the recording and deleted the call from the records.

Jack thanked her and resumed his story. "Christi felt that there was only one way the demons could make it seem like the shield worked to stop the missile under the super tight security and review of the rocket and the launch personnel would be to "cause" the "abort" signal be sent from the launch control desk. That would make the rocket explode and the test would be seen as a success. Trying to block the signal is virtually impossible. So immediately after liftoff a 6.4 Magnitude earthquake hit the area of the launch site and completely destroyed the launch facility. No abort signal could be sent, so, the missile struck the target and the shield was shown to be a failure."

Iris asked, "What if the demons could cause the abort signal receiver on the missile to think it received a signal?"

Jack came back, "We thought of that possibility. First, demons aren't good at advanced weaponry and we believed they had used the signal method on the earlier tests and would think it would also work this time. Second, the "Abort" signal is only created and set during the launch sequence by the console and matched to the receiver on the missile."

Iris thought for a second, "And if they had "induced" the launch officer to send the signal, the earthquake would have prevented that also. I suppose that there was a "harp" involved in this?"

Jack said, "Anything is possible Iris, but then you'd know more about that than I would."

Iris laughed, "Well, all's well as it worked out, we want to thank you and your team even if no one else knows about your part in it. Also, just between us, Israel would have given the Russians an actual demonstration of their shield's flaws before they threatened the world, if you hadn't shown them first. Your way was a much better solution. Slalom."

Jack noted the call for further discussion with the Core Team the next day. Then he and Laura called the day done and they headed for their compartment to get some sleep.

They used the eye print/biomass system to enter their rooms and each of them grabbed a shower before retiring.

The two room suite of rooms had been carefully designed to be as close as physically possible to their apartment in the undersea base. It came very close to the original design except it was significantly more compact due to shipboard constraints.

Still, the bed was similar in shape and comfort and the illusion of a sea breeze blowing in gently through open French doors was maintained so it felt the same. Laura nestled up next to Jack's bigger frame as he wrapped her up in his arms. They fell asleep quickly.

It seemed like he had just fallen asleep when he was awoken by a presence in the dark room. He reached out and clicked on the room lights. Jack immediately recognized the Angel Caleb in his old man persona. He checked the time and realized he had actually gotten four hours' sleep. He looked at the Angel. "Greetings, Caleb, what can we do for you at this early hour?"

Caleb smiled slightly. "I'm sorry I awakened you. Not needing sleep sometimes causes one to forget, that as mortals you do require it. My apologies although the message I bear is important, I could have waited until later."

Laura asked, "What is the message Hugo?"

The eons-old Angel stared through her for a bit before he spoke. "Since you have just resolved a particularly tense time and deadline with the Russian manipulation by Satan's forces, it would behoove us to grant you a period of rest before taxing your team again. Alas, it seems that is not to be. A new effort by the demonic forces is threatening believers in Yahshua in the Far East, more precisely, China. The enemy of man and angels is convincing the Premier of that huge country that the rhetoric of Marco Marino is right in the hatred of Yahshua's followers as the cause of the disappearance of millions of people world-wide. In a warped way they are tying the disappearance as an operation of aliens working in tandem with Christians. The most compelling proof they use is your team."

"Our team?" exclaimed Laura. "How do the demons use our team to mislead the Chinese Premier?"

Hugo shrugged his shoulders in a very human gesture, "Your Field Generators, your invulnerability, your ship, your aircraft. They are beyond Earth's ability to attain or create them. The demons tell the Premier that those things are alien. They *are* from outside of this world because they are from God. To a lifetime non-believer, the idea that they are from an advanced race of aliens is far easier to believe than an all-powerful deity and it is only a small jump that the Premier believes primarily because he thinks that he thought of the concept himself, when it was actually whispered into his ear while he was asleep."

Hugo sighed, another very human expression. "As for your mission it will be one that will stretch your capabilities farther than ever before. You will need to stay unknown and free until you can convince the Premier of China that God is real and that demons and Marco Marino are behind the alien scam instead of the reality of the Lord calling forth the true believers."

Jack asked, "What is the timeline for this mission?"

Hugo stared at Jack briefly. "The sooner you can accomplish this mission the less people will be persecuted and killed in China. A warning though, Zhou Tangtao cannot get involved or the demons will reveal his conversion to Yahshua to the Premier and, he will be killed."

Jack shook his head, "Great." But, his face lit up with a new concept as his mind explored the thought.

CHAPTER TWENTY-SIX

The entire Core Group considered the new mission and how to accomplish it. After a great amount of ideas and concepts were looked at and rejected as unworkable, they began to pray and seek Heaven's help.

They had prayed, praised, and worshipped and Jack was about to present their quandary when Raquel appeared. Jack smiled at the powerful Archangel, "Welcome mighty warrior, have you come to shed clarity on our problem?"

"Yes I have. Now hear the word of the Most High Elohim." *"Jack Malone, you have discerned the only possible solution to this dilemma. Take your wife, Christi, Elon, Ariella, Charlie Wu, Su Li, and Megan Cole as they each have a skill that will be needed to both survive and accomplish the mission. Raquel and Rose will be watching. Be courageous and I will bless your efforts."*

After they prayed their thanks to Yahveh in Yahshua's name, Mark commented, "Have you been holding out on us? What "Solution" do you have secreted in your mind that we haven't covered?" Mark's grin took the sting out of his words.

Jack shook his head, "I did not mention a thought I had because it was like we would be playing God and we all know that doesn't work. Zhou Tangtao's life is on the chopping block if he gets involved in this delusion driving the Premier. The Premier is practically inaccessible and will never give up power to God. But, what if Zhou became Premier?"

Mark chewed on that for a bit and nodded his head. "Yes, I see that. He is next in line to be Premier and because of his walk with Yahshua the demons can't possess him. He would defuse this garbage about aliens and stop the persecution of the Christians too. But, and it is a BIG but, how are the eight of you, not Chinese, but outsiders going to ferment a coup'?"

"Jack shrugged, "I have no idea but I believe the Father will guide us in all righteousness to accomplish His Will."

Mark nodded again, "I'm sure He will. So. This time you guys have an away trip and the rest of us will hold down the fort, or in this case, the ship."

Jack grinned, "You and Sarah can run things here until we return. I'll notify everyone from the General and the Prime Minister down of your authority. Three things I would like you to do for me during our absence. First, don't start a world war, second, leave the Chinese alone, if possible, and third, review the rank and file and promote those who deserve it after praying about it. Good enough?

Mark nodded, "No problem with those requests, except if you run into trouble I will ignore the second requirement which could start the problem stated in the first requirement."

Jack laughed, "Well, I certainly hope so."

After Mark departed for the SOG area, Jack called Laura, Christi, Elon, Ariella, Charlie, Su Li, and Megan Cole. Everyone was dressed in generic clothing that would allow them to fit into the normal Chinese population and not draw attention.

They planned their unannounced, illegal, and unwanted entrance into the Chinese mainland for the next evening. Tomorrow would allow them time to get into disguise and travel. Jack then explained his plan to achieve the Father's goals. Their first act would be to contact an old friend, Han Le, a comrade in arms who was an ex-Chinese commando turned Christian from an earlier excursion into China.

Before they scattered for the evening Jack mentioned several limitations they faced on this trip. "We won't be able to take our Field Generators with us. As far as I can figure, we shouldn't have contact with the demons afflicting the Premier, so we probably won't need our armor, shields, and swords. That will put us back to square one. We will have our skills, courage, and prayer to accomplish our goals."

Jack and Laura prayed over the troops and dismissed them. "Get some good sleep tonight. I doubt that tomorrow night's accommodations will be as nice."

After the other people left, and the Angels disappeared, Jack and Laura remained and prayed some more for God's provision, protection, and support for everyone going on this trip.

Later after they retired to their suite of rooms, Jack mentioned, "This is obviously going to be a rough trip because the Father is protecting us not only an Angel but also an Archangel."

Laura smiled and hugged him tightly, "We'll be fine my love, remember we're in a win-win situation."

Jack thought about her words and slowly nodded his head. "You're right, I'm still thinking like a non-believer. Forgive me Father, I confess my fear as sin, the sin of unbelief in your plans and provision, and I ask you to forgive me in Yahshua's name.

In the mess hall, Christi, Elon, Ariella, Charlie, Su Li, and Megan Cole sat discussing tomorrows' trip. Charlie deferred the leadership of the group to Christi because he felt led by the Father to do that regardless of his greater age and experience.

Christi raised the question of what were their unique skills and how they would use them. The discussion ranged widely about the possibilities. Eventually they headed off to their quarters to get as much sleep as they could. Elon and Charlie were the last to leave and Elon asked, "Why didn't you lead the discussion here?"

Charlie smiled slightly, "I was led to let Christi lead this time."

Elon frowned slightly, "I'd think your greater experience would have been more practical as the leader."

Charlie laughed at that, "I've done a lot of things, but no one in this team, including me, has ever held a sword to the throat of Satan himself to judge him and decide to kill him or let him live. Christi did that, which says a lot about God's trust in her and you'd do well to remember that. Goodnight Elon, see you in the morning."

Elon stood there stunned. His thought was "I need to learn to keep my mouth shut more often."

The next morning, the away team was expertly disguised by a working group of Alexis, David, and Linda Wu. All experts trained in the spy arts they transformed the non-Chinese into looking more Chinese. When Elon became impatient Linda Wu grabbed him by his chin in an iron grip and said, "Be still! You should be glad you're not being disguised as a Japanese. Because we'd have to bob your nose and that can really hurt."

CHAPTER TWENTY-SEVEN

After receiving detailed instructions on how to maintain their new looks and repair them if necessary, the travelers had a quick class on Chinese dos and don'ts and reminded that illegal entry into China was a hanging offense.

Using his encrypted cell phone, which he had left with Zhou Tangtao, Jack learned of Han Le's location and how to contact him.

Alexis handed out the correct paperwork for each person in the event they were stopped. Everyone practiced their Chinese name until it became comfortable. Then they were ready to leave.

The Sword had sailed submerged to a location a hundred miles off of the coast of China. It surfaced and launched one of the "Fragment" aircraft with its Force Generator in the special mode, which made it invisible to the naked eye. The plane was extremely stealthy to begin with and with the FG absorbing any radar or laser energies there were no reflected signals. Essentially, it wasn't detectable.

The autonomous ship selected a deserted building within a mile of Han Le's location and disembarked the eight team members and then lifted off and was gone.

Jack contacted Han Le and the group casually slipped out of the building and into the sparse foot traffic on a side street. They walked somewhat apart until they reached a tea house. Most of the group sat outside and acted like they were waiting for someone or simply killing some time.

Jack and Charlie entered the Tea Shop and they stopped at a remote table where Han Le stood up to greet them.

Following Chinese custom Han Le bowed his head and smiled at Jack and Charlie who smiled back and bowed to Han Le. The three men sat down and talked quietly together over cups of Jasmine tea.

Han Le shook his head and spoke in the Mandarin language. "I never expected to see you again my old friend, especially here and looking so Chinese. It is a great honor.

Speaking the same language Jack smiled at Han Le. "I am also honored to see you once again. Allow me to introduce Zhijian Chochim, my friend and fellow warrior."

Han and Charlie exchanged greetings and then Han looked at Jack. "Peace be to you both in the name of Yahshua. May His blessings cover you while you are here in this troubled land."

Jack again bowed, "And the same to you Han Le. How are you faring in your new life?"

Han Le sighed, "Until recently I have been doing well, planting new churches and mentoring new believers in the true faith. But, things have become very grim in the last few months. The government is carrying on like the pogroms of the past, detaining believers everywhere and putting them into prison as if they are terrorists. They are never heard from again. The government has spies everywhere and the people are afraid to be associated with us for fear of arrest. There is no appeal of the arrests. And I am afraid they have their eyes on me and it won't be long before they ask me if I am a Christian. I trust the Lord and I will not deny my Savior. You are endangering yourselves by meeting with me. You could be arrested also. I am sorry that I have to tell you this but it would have been better if you had stayed away from me."

Jack looked at Charlie who asked, "We are fairly familiar with the persecution of our faith. Han, have you spoken to Zhou about this?"

Han shook his head, "No, I was warned not to expose him and his faith because it will mean the end for him if I do."

Charlie asked, "Who warned you Han?"

Han smiled, "A beautiful Angel came to me in a dream several nights ago and spoke to me."

Jack casually looked around while the other two were talking and realized that there was trouble building in the tea house. There was a dozen new "customers" who weren't ordering anything and the earlier customers had quietly left the tea house. He tapped quietly on the table to get the attention of the other two. It was obviously a trap which was about to be sprung.

Jack spoke quietly, "Raquel, I think we are about to be arrested in here."

The door to the tea house opened and the Archangel stepped into the room and casually walked back to the trio at the back of the room.

Raquel walked over to Jack and said in a quiet voice, "We need to leave immediately."

The three men got up and walked out of the tea house. None of the others tried to stop them or said a word to them.

Outside, things were normal with people coming and going. Jack looked at Han and winked, "It seems you were right about the eyes on you and that your reputation has preceded you."

Han said to Jack, "How were you able to get us out of there?"

Jack tipped his head toward Raquel, "You'll have to ask him."

The Angel Rose gathered the team members and herded them along with Han away from the tea house and around the nearest corner and down the side street.

Raquel spoke to Jack, "We are being pressured by a demonic force that is eroding our control over the government forces. We need to hide you from physical view so that the Most High can shield us all from the view of the demons."

Laura nodded her head, "Raquel, how long can the Father keep us out of the sight of the demons?"

Raquel laughed softly. "As long as he wishes. But, there are other things that are involved and you will all be arrested and taken to jail for a time. We will be right next door, dimensionally speaking."

Jack understood the Archangels dilemma and waved the Angels away quickly. As they disappeared, a bunch of Chinese troops suddenly appeared at both ends of the alley they were in.

Jack quietly said, "Don't fight them, let them arrest us. This is God's Will for right now."

The troops surrounded them, searched them, and then, handcuffed them and transported them to a local police station.

After they had all been placed in two cells, men in one and the women in the other, their handcuffs were removed and they were locked in.

Charlie looked at Jack and shook his head, "Fine state of affairs, I don't see this as improving our chances to change the regime very much."

Jack nodded, "I understand your concern. Trust the Lord."

CHAPTER TWENTY-EIGHT

As the guards left the area of the cells, one thin man stood there in his uniform, staring at the prisoners. The lower part of Thu Chang's face was twisted somewhat to the right of center and there was some barely visible scarring in that area. Looking in his eyes an experienced observer would see barely suppressed intense anger. The stare was a glare and a hint of violent satisfaction in their incarceration. He stepped closer to the cell with the women in it. Smiling, he spoke in good English that was somewhat distorted by his injury to his face. "Well, well, Mrs. Malone, it seems that I was correct that you were going to my jail. Where I will "squeeze" the secrets of your power and your ship out of you, your husband, and the rest of you decadent Americans!"

Laura walked over to the bars and coolly looked at their jailer. "You were wrong the first time you attempted to arrest me and you are wrong again. These powers and ship you speak of are from God and are never going to be yours."

Thu Chang laughed a cruel laugh. "You've just condemned yourself and these with you. By order of the Premier all Christians who won't deny their false religion will be put to death. By me!

Laura wanted to be afraid but knew better. God brought them to this point and he would see them through it. She didn't have a force generator field to protect her this time but she wasn't going to ever deny her Savior or His father. She steeled herself for the upcoming torture.

All at once she felt herself being moved aside and looked back to see Christi moving up to the bars in her place.

Christi smiled at the man. "Perhaps you'll take me first as an example to possibly change Mrs. Malone's mind? I figure you're going to get around to me soon or later. Why not now?"

Jack, Laura, Elon, Ariella, Charlie, Su Li, Megan Cole, and even Han Le all started a clamor against that idea.

Seeing the dread and anxiety on those faces encouraged the man's selection. "Very well, I'm sure your screams will be very helpful in my education of these people." He called three guards to escort the younger female into the next room where he would interrogate her. He eyed her full figure and her beauty with a lustful smile. After she was out of the cell and the door was locked again he ran his hand over her body and asked, "Do you have any last words for her friends."

Christi turned and looked at the mournful looks on their faces and smiled, "Now, don't worry about me, I can still claim those bonuses you know." She turned and with her head held high she walked across the floor to the door and went through it.

The man whose name was Thu Chang, liked her subservient nature told most of the guards to stay in the cell area randomly took two guards into the torture room with him.

Laura shook her head and looked at Jack. She was shocked to see him smiling. "Doesn't it bother you at all that that maniac is going to molest and torture Christi to death?"

Jack shook his head, "Nope, not at all. Remember her last words? She's got this. I don't know how, but I know she's got this under control."

Just then there was a long keening scream of terror from the next room that raised the hairs on everybody's neck. That was followed by continuous garbled screams and mumbled pleas for mercy. There were more screams and two loud thumps. Then all was quiet and the silence was even more ominous.

Laura looked back to Jack and he was still smiling. She didn't know what to think and started to pray. A peace came over her that silenced the fear and worry for Christi. She relaxed and waited.

After what seemed like a long time, the door opened and nobody came out. Several of the guards raised their rifles and entered the room. There were three more loud thumps before silence ensued. Then Christi walked out of the room and headed to the cells with a set of keys in her hand. The remaining three guards yelled at her to stop. When she ignored them they opened fire on her.

Christi stopped and looked at the three men and suddenly they flew backwards through the air and smashed into the far wall. From the amount of blood each man left on the wall there wasn't any doubt they were dead. Christi unlocked both of the cells and everyone mobbed her. Jack restored order finally and asked Christi, "Where's your body armor and your green LED?"

She smiled, "Don't need them."

Jack frowned and continued to stare at her. Christi sighed, "Okay, it is the way I understand God's protection. I knew he wouldn't leave us defenseless. Our armor, swords and shields don't need the force generators to work, we just pray and they appear. Why not the force generator fields?"

Jack shook his head, "It's as clear as day now that you have stated it. God complimented our shaky faith in Him by using our existing faith in technology to give us the strength we needed to use the fields. Now, we've moved closer to Him and our faith is stronger. Was this the first time you have done it strictly on faith alone?"

Christi shook her head, "Nope, I haven't used the blue switch in our last three battles. I prayed in the name and the blood of Yahshua that the Father would protect me with the force generator field. Then I felt that tingly feeling all over. I knew in my heart that the Father had empowered me with the defense field."

Laura asked, "What was that terrible screaming we heard from that room, and all that muffled pleading for mercy?"

Christi shrugged her shoulders. "Thu Chang went insane when he tried to cut me with a scalpel and he couldn't hurt me. To him it was a reenactment of what happened to him when he attacked Laura in the store. His mind couldn't handle another failure and he lost his mind, never to find it again. He tried, several more times to hurt me and that didn't work. One of his soldiers tried to calm him down. He went into a full rage and attacked the guard. The guard, apparently, had all he wanted of a crazy man and ran Thu Chang through with his bayonet. He must have hit Chang's heart because he folded up and dropped dead to the floor."

"The other two guards didn't understand why the first guard killed their supervisor so they killed the first guard with their bayonets. At that point they decided to attack me for causing everything. I "saw" them flying into the outer wall and the field did exactly that. Then three more guards came in and were going to shoot me. They joined their fellow guards in death. I then came out here."

Jack looked at Laura. "Why don't we retire and let Christi run the Team? She is moving on a higher level than we are and it could be a benefit for all of us."

Christi laughed and shook her head. "No chance. Yahshua told me, personally, that you two were going to head up this team until He calls us all home. I don't have your experience or your abilities. I'm just doing my part to help the team. But... I do have a suggestion."

Jack grinned, "Pray tell us of this new revelation."

Christi grinned back at him. "Let's all get back in our cells after we put the key back in the pocket one of the guards and lock ourselves in."

Ariella looked at Christi, "Why? Why do we want to do that?"

Jack answered her, "Because it will remove any thought by whoever investigates the slaughter that we could have had any part in the murders. I'm not sure how that will help our situation in the near future."

Christi nodded her head making the hair of her black wig fly around her face. "Instead of being on the run with everybody in China hunting us we could bide our time to strike where it will do the most good."

Charlie Wu spoke up, "Actually, we could do that, but I think I understand the Chinese mindset pretty good. Let's go back in the cells but leave the doors open. When the relief force comes they will find us capable but not interested in escaping. That will muddy the waters sufficiently to bring our presence to a higher level and possibly to the Premier himself."

Jack nodded, "Good thought Charlie, I think we could do that right now since we can use the defensive shield as needed." Jack looked around, "Since Christi told us how to pray for the field, by a show of hands, how many have tried it and found that it works?"

Everybody raised a hand. Except Jack himself. "All right, Charlie get one of the guard's radios and ask for some room service. Oh, and ask them to bring six body bags."

CHAPTER TWENTY-NINE

Charlie made the call and everyone prayed for their defensive field just in case. Jack told Han Le to stay behind one of them if there was any shooting.

Less than ten minutes later, a twenty-five-man force of Chinese Commandos rushed into the room armed to the teeth and surrounded the Team. Han Le didn't have anywhere to hide so he simply acted as calm as the others.

An officer with the rank of Colonel walked forward and stood in front of Han Le. "Commander Le, although you have been relieved of your rank and branded a traitor I remember our times together and the battles we won. Although I am not being politically correct, I still think of you as my friend."

Han Le bowed his head in agreement. The Colonel asked, "Would you please tell me what has happened here?"

Han Le looked at Jack. He turned back to the officer. "Colonel Trang, it is nice to see you again. You have done well in the Commando Service. I am going to refer you to my good friend, Jack Malone, as he is more familiar with these events than am I."

Careful not to make any sudden moves, Jack stepped over to the Officer. Speaking in Mandarin Jack addressed the man. "Good afternoon Colonel, as my friend Han Le said, I am Jack Malone of the Crossfire Team. I can tell you what transpired here. One of the Chinese Army officers, Captain Thu Chang, went insane in attempting to interrogate one of our people. As he was unable to hurt her he turned on one of the guards who defended himself and killed the Captain in self-defense. The other two guards then killed the first guard and turned on the prisoner at which time the power of God threw them against the wall, killing them. Three more guards entered the interrogation room and sought to shoot the prisoner and suffered the same fate as the first two. We called for additional guards to replace the ones who died."

The Colonel was impressed. He did not detect any falsehood in the leader of the Crossfire Team or his story. He looked at the taller Caucasian. "Very well General Malone. I accept your version of things but I have no way to report these "acts of God" to my superiors. How would you suggest I word that part of my report?"

Jack smiled, "I would use, "unknown forces beyond the scope of this report", it seems to work in America and the Middle East."

The Colonel nodded his head. "Thank you General Malone, I am officially releasing you and the people with you on my authority. You are free to go." The Colonel looked around and directed his Commandos back to their barracks. Before he left he smiled at Jack. In English he said, "Before anymore actions occur that are by "unknown forces beyond the scope of this report"." He shook Jack's hand and nodded to Han before he walked away.

Han moved up next to Jack. "The Colonel is smart, I trained him well. He could tell he couldn't hurt any of you but you could do immense harm to him and the country. What do we do now?"

Jack said, "Let's get out of here before the Colonel gets overruled. Then we need to pray for guidance."

Laura and Christi said, "Amen" at the same time.

A half hour later they found a secluded park and they all sat on the grass and prayed to Yahveh God for direction.

There wasn't any response, but when Jack opened his eyes he saw the Angels Raquel and Rose sitting quietly among the team members.

Laura asked, "Hello again Angels, any words as to our next direction?"

Rose smiled, "We're here to assist you in any way you need. But, the prosecution of this mission is entirely up to you."

Jack had been reviewing the on-going history of the Crossfire Team's successes and began to see a possibility for their mission this time.

Jack called Raquel and Rose over to his position. "Raquel, I believe that there are a large number of Mizrahi, or Oriental Jews, right?"

The Archangel nodded his head. Jack smiled, "Tell us about them, please."

Raquel was intrigued by this line of reasoning. "Certainly, the Mizrahi Jews, are also referred to as Edot HaMizrach Communities of the East; Mizrahi Hebrew or "Sons of the East" or Oriental Jews, are Jews descended from local Jewish communities of the Middle East. The term Mizrahi is most commonly used in Israel to refer to Jews who trace their roots back to Muslim-majority countries. This includes descendants of Babylonian Jews and Mountain Jews from modern Iraq, Syria, Bahrain, Kuwait, Dagestan, Azerbaijan, Iran, Lebanon, Uzbekistan, Caucasus, Kurdistan, Afghanistan and Pakistan. Also, Yemenite, Turkish and Persian Jews are usually included within the Mizrahi Jewish group. The term Mizrahim often consists of Maghrebi Jews, including the Sephardic who lived in North Africa."

Jack thought about that and then gave the Archangel a specific task to do. Raquel disappeared only to reappear twenty minutes later with a sheath of documents, which he showed to Jack. Since most of the papers were in Chinese he could read them easily.

Jack thanked him and sat down with the other team mates. "I think we have a game changer here." He pointed at the papers. The present Premier of China has a little secret he doesn't want disclosed to his opponents or the mass of Chinese people either."

Laura spoke up. "What do those papers prove, Jack?"

"That Premier Zhang is of Jewish descent. These papers show his paternal tree and that dates back to a Jewish community that existed in Kaifeng since the Northern Song Dynasty circa 960 to 1127. Kaifeng, then the capital of the Northern Song Dynasty, was a cosmopolitan city on a branch of the Silk Road. It is surmised that a small community of Jews, most likely from Persia settled there."

Jack smiled, "Raquel, did you confirm that Premier Zhang has the correct DNA that confirms his Jewishness?"

Raquel looked through Jack for several seconds. "Yes, he has the true DNA."

Jack studied the Archangel a bit. "Did the demons directing the Premier give you any problems?"

Raquel shrugged his shoulders, "They tried to prevent me from finding those papers. The ones that didn't die fled back to their dimension. I don't think they will come back, ever."

Charlie Wu asked Jack, "Okay, how does this help us? You know the Premier won't accept the fact that his ancient ancestors were Jews has any bearing on him today. His dedication to Maoism and the atheism of the country is all he has ever known; so why will he care?"

Jack smiled at Charlie, "Of all the members of the Team I would think you would truly realize the power of one's ancestors against the Maoism of today's Chinese leaders."

Charlie shook his head, "Thanks to Mao that's changed. When the ancestral temples were destroyed most families lost the records of their extended family. This has led to a major shift in China, family is now seen as the three living generations, beyond that is largely forgotten. A friend of mine is a devout communist, but the loss of his family's history is one act that he never forgave Mao for. The temples have not been rebuilt, and most ancestor worship has disappeared."

Raquel spoke up, "While that is true for the common Chinese person on the street, the advantaged and wealthy were able to keep their temples and shrines and now consider it a privileged right of the "noble" class to revere and pray to their ancestors. Premier Zhang came from a wealthy family and his ancestors are, and have been, important to him. This fact is unknown to almost everyone else but his family."

Charlie frowned, "I know I'm sounding like a nay-sayer but, how does that help us?"

CHAPTER THIRTY

Jack smiled, "Because, with the help from our Archangel friend, Raquel, Premier Zhang is going to have a meeting tonight with one of his influential forefathers in a dream, or awake. His forefather will convince him to step down and follow another path. He will also convince the, soon to retire Premier, that he should promote the right person to be the next Premier to the President of China who is a personal friend and ally of Zhang."

Charlie frowned a bit and then smiled and nodded his head. "That could work. If the President wants Zhang's selection to stand, then that person will become the next Premier of Security for the nation of China."

Jack turned to Raquel, "Is that something you can do within Heaven's rules?"

The Archangel slowly nodded his head. "I've already discussed this action with Hugo and he reluctantly agreed with the premise. When do you want me to speak to the Premier as his forefather?"

Jack thought the entire operation through again and said, "Tonight and the next four nights if needed."

"Consider it done." Raquel disappeared and Jack turned to talk with the other team members.

Raquel reappeared with a monumental frown on his face. He shook his head and stared at Jack. "We need to change our approach. It seems that Satan saw what we did to the Russian President and has prepared Premier Zhang for this specific form of interference by the Crossfire Team, working through Angelic forces. I did some subconscious sampling to see how Zhang would respond to a visit by his forefathers. The demonic has conditioned his mind to reject all but the strongest effort concerning control of the man through his worship of his ancestors. They have trained him that he must commit suicide if the pressure exceeds his conditioning. And, as a backup they have continual teams of demons to make sure he does just that as soon as they sense our involvement."

Charlie asked, "Can they do that legally?"

Raquel turned his golden eyes on the Asian man. "Zhang has done many things and opened many doors to his soul. The demonic has had legal access for decades to his spiritual life to build heavily-rooted strongholds. Yes, they do have the legal right to oppress him as they want because he let them in."

Jack shook his head, "I had a feeling it was all too easy. Now we are back to step one again.

Jack prayed quietly in his mind. "Father Yahveh, in the name of your son, Yahshua, I pray for your guidance in this mission. Satan is stepping up his defenses against us and I am not sure how to overcome their forces. Lead me Father."

As he waited for that guidance he wondered what Mark would do in this case. He realized that *this thought was his guidance.* He smiled and looked at Raquel. "Okay, if they want to play hardball we've all been trained by Mark in what to do. What is the best way to get the demonic forces to attack us?"

Christi answered, "Make a move in the physical on the Premier. That should excite the demons. They're bound to try something stupid before Satan can stop them."

Charlie grinned, "I do like the way this woman thinks, are you sure she's not related to Mark? Let's spice it up with a planned assault on the demons controlling the Premier as if we're going to drive them off and spoil their plans. That should result in a full court press to destroy us. And they don't know we have our defense field because we don't have our body armor."

Jack asked Laura, Elon, Ariella, Su Li, Megan Cole, and Han Le, if they had anything to add to the concept. They did not, so the planning started for an assault on the Premier.

The next morning at six a.m., the eight members of the away team approached the residence of Premier where the Angel Rose assured them he was this early in the day.

The plan was so designed so they would not to actually see the Premier but to make his controlling demons think they were going to see him. That part of their plan worked really well. They were entering the part of the neighborhood where the Premier's home was when they were confronted by three demons who were prepared to fight. Jack prayed for the defensive field and was rewarded with the tingly feeling over his whole body. But the demons simply stood there blocking the way. This was very strange behavior for demons of any kind.

Jack was about to move on the demons when a large, very high level demon appeared and addressed Jack directly. "Puny human, my Master wants you to know that we are aware we can't defeat you with the armor you possess. So, we will kill ten humans in this area for each one of you every minute you continue to interfere in our business. You need to leave now or it will be on your heads for the slaughter."

Jack was praying the whole time the demon was talking and it disappeared just as Raquel appeared next to Jack. The Archangel smiled at the Team members. Through Raquel, God told the Arch demon to, *"Tell your Master that I will not permit this evil. If Satan persists in following through with it, then, I will release the Crossfire warriors who will be given access to your domain with their armor and specific instructions to hunt him down and kill him. Immediately!"*

Jack asked, "What happened then?"

Raquel laughed, "The statement rattled the Arch demon and he was unsure of what to do. He knew if he took that message to his Master, it would result in his own death. But not to tell Satan would be even worse. So to protect himself he told the three demons to take the message to Satan."

"The Arch demon and all three of the messenger demons were never seen again after the message was delivered to Satan. But it has interfered with your plan to engage the demons around the Premier. They have warned him that your team is here and you mean to kill him. He is presently calling out everyone to hunt you down and stop you. With your defense fields that is not a real problem, but, they've gotten him to flee to a safe hideout and we have not been able to find him yet due to their interference.

CHAPTER THIRTY-ONE

Jack sat down on a large rock in the small park they had found. He gave his frustration to Yahshua and asked for guidance. "Yahshua, you know our situation and our mission. I ask for your leading on how we can achieve the Father's Will in this matter. We need your direction as we are not able to see our way to do this and must lean on your strength to prevent more needless deaths of our Chinese brothers and sisters."

He rested quietly, knowing that God would grant him an answer in His time. He sensed a presence and looked up to see Caleb in his awesome Angelic form standing in front of him.

Caleb nodded to Jack and spoke in a deep bass voice. "Jack Malone, the Most High God has heard your plea and was moved. Now hear the word of God. *"Jack, I understand your situation and will give you what you ask for because you are truly My Son in your heart and in your will. Satan has decided to do everything in his power to defeat you in this matter. It is his right to do this thing. But, that does not mean you are defeated or have to bow to his will. To change the ongoing slaughter of my children in China I am giving your team the power to seek out the devil and convince him to give up this effort and release his control of the Chinese Premier completely or you will destroy his kingdom and if necessary, destroy him. To accomplish this goal, I will give each member of your team the protective field and further, Jack I will give you alone the power you used to destroy Xndalius, if and when you need it. Also, Christi has a recent history with Satan that he won't soon forget. Go in My Power and Love. My Angels and I will be with you on this quest."*

Jack looked at Caleb, "This mission from God is huge in consequences and potential for us. I, we, are going to need Angelic support in all phases of it, will you be with us?"

Caleb smiled, "If that is your desire then all three of us will be with you". As he spoke, the Angels Raquel and Rose appeared behind him.

Jack nodded his head. He turned to the other team members with a large sigh. "You are all aware of the huge responsibilities and dangers this "quest" puts on us. I will not judge anyone here who wants to sit this one out. You each have to know in your heart that this could well be your final job in this life. How say each of you, what is your choice?"

Christi said, "I'm going with you to the end. Which really isn't an end, but, you know what I mean."

Laura added, "Me too." The others agreed with Laura. Charlie laughed, "The ultimate Road Trip. Who wouldn't want to go?"

Jack looked at them all, "Any reasonably sane person to start with. I really appreciate your responses. Now, let's huddle with our support group and figure out where to begin."

Raquel spoke for the Angels. "We must go to the Demonic dimension to seek out Satan. To do this places us three Angelic warriors of God in a lose-lose situation. In that dimension we cannot hide from the demons and they will attack us with as many demons as it takes to overwhelm us and destroy us. Still, we gave you our word that we will fight alongside of you and that is what we'll do as long as we have strength."

Christi shook her head, "No! you three are members of this mission just as the rest of us. God said, *"To accomplish this goal, I will give each member of your team the protective field."* That means you can also have the protective field of God's grace that the mightiest demon cannot penetrate. You will also be indestructible as we are."

Jack was awed by Christi's insight and prayed to God to confirm her interpretation. God spoke in Jacks mind. *"She is correct; without the field my Angelic warriors would have no chance in the Demonic kingdom."*

Jack looked at Raquel, "Christi is right; God will provide you with the protective field in the Demonic Kingdom because of the unbalance of the three of you against all the demons of hell."

Raquel turned his golden look to Christi. "I, and my fellow Angels, thank you for your heart's passion for us."

Christi smiled in response. "You are most welcome mighty Angel. I am pleased we could help you."

Jack had been praying and announced, "To make this Quest work we need to go to his realm and start destroying enough of his kingdom that he will be forced to deal with us personally. Raquel where is his most treasured or critical operations?"

Raquel laughed, "You and Mark Connelly are a lot alike, Jack. At present, the devil's most important workshop is an area where the war against Israel is created and controlled. There are very old programs and brand new ones with a thousand years of devilment in between those two. If you, like Mark, want to incite Satan to uncontrollable rage this is the place to attack. You will definitely get his personal attention."

Jack looked at his fellow teammates, "Pray for your defensive fields now before we go." He asked Han Le to pray for them while they were gone and to hide himself until they returned." Han Le nodded his head and wished them God's favor on their quest.

Raquel saw that everyone was ready and prayed for a direct transfer to the region of hell that was their target.

CHAPTER THIRTY-TWO

The calm skies over China disappeared and were replaced by a dimly lit darkness with highlights in the red end of the spectrum. Hundreds of demon were doing mostly incomprehensible things or scurrying around to accomplish their duties. All eight of the humans were encased in their armor and shields with their swords at the ready. The three Angels drew their swords. Jack checked with Raquel to ensure all three of the Angels were protected by the defensive fields before the fireworks started.

Jack pointed at the busiest place he could see and headed for it. As they advanced Christi got a word from Yahveh as to the legal correctness of their quest.

Suddenly, it was as if every creature in sight knew they were there and stopped what they were doing and turned to look at the eleven trespassers. Maybe one or two hundred of the demons dropped what they were doing and charged toward the team, wielding every conceivable form of weapon.

The wave of demons crashed into the line of human and Angel warriors, literally hell-bent on killing them. Nothing they did harmed the invaders. But, the opposite was not so. The Team eliminated every demon within reach and charged more of them driven by a Holy anger that was increasing with every step. The real destroyers were the Angels. Protected for the first time in their history, they applied their centuries of battle experience against their enemy with immense passion. For every demon eliminated by the eight humans, each Angel took out three or four.

Full of anger and slow of wit as they were, it did not take the remaining demons too long to realize they were not winning this battle. Before long, the demons were fleeing the Team as quickly as possible. Jack continued to move into the beehive of activity noting it was obvious that not all demons were aware of their presence. In each area the Team started destroying the occupied demons and then repelled a force of several hundred demons until those that remained fled. Their armor and swords disappeared.

After six such events Charlie suggested they stop and eat something before they ran out of energy killing demons.

Jack was still recovering his breath and looked around, "Good idea, Charlie, did you happen to see a good restaurant along the way? Possibly a drive through?"

Elon spoke up, "We didn't think to bring food, why was that?"

Jack sighed, "Because I never thought it would take this long to get Satan's attention."

Laura, Christi, Ariella, Su Li, and Megan Cole all offered some power bars they had brought along. Jack said, "Thanks. Fine dining never tasted better."

As they finished up eating, there was a tremendous crash of thunder, multiple lightning strikes, a cloud of red smoke and Satan appeared before them. Immediately the armor and shield of God along with the sword of power appeared on all eight humans.

The dominate evil in the universe was obviously unhappy with them. In uncontrolled anger he pointed one finger at the group. "You are trespassing in my domain and I have the legal right to destroy you. He created a massive ball of pure energy and threw it at the team. Everything around them exploded, melted, or disappeared. When it was over they were still standing there staring at him. He created More balls of energy and threw them at the team with the same results.

Jack could swear that he could see steam coming out of the devil's ears he was so mad. Jack held up one hand, "Stop wasting our time! You can't hurt us. We're here at God's command to offer you a choice."

Satan stopped attacking them. "I know why you're here. I am not going to stop bending the Defense Premier to my will no matter what you do. Anyway, you all are about to die and stop bothering me. Your God's protection fields are about to fail. I will bring such unrighteousness against you even that level of righteousness will be overcome!"

Jack laughed, "These fields are backed with the power that created the entire universe. What simpleton convinced you could beat that?"

Hearing the all-powerful reference to God made Satan so mad he became angry beyond belief. "The Trifect of Si-Ogny that's who! It knows more about the laws of both the natural and the, so-called, supernatural dimensions than your puny God ever has!"

Jack smiled, "Oh, him. You had better check your facts before you bet your entire kingdom and your life on the word of an alien charlatan. Release China and the Premier completely now or we will prevail and tear down your kingdom until we terminate you."

Satan was about to scoff at Jack's statement until he saw the woman Christi standing near Jack. He heard the word "Remember" again. That rattled him and stole his confidence.

"I will think on this. You will have your answer in one day." Satan disappeared quietly and with no fanfare this time.

All the other demons left them alone. Jack told Raquel to take them to a safe place. They were all suddenly in a large room in the third heaven.

The Angel Hugo appeared and was given the story up until the present time. He disappeared briefly and then returned.

He looked at the eight humans and the three Angels and knew the what he had to say would not change their minds nor their duty to God's Quest they were on. These were some of the few humans he knew who were bold as lions and humble as doves. Hugo spoke. "I discussed this with the Most High and what Satan said is partially true. If Satan can bring to bear enough unrighteousness he could overcome one of the defensive fields you have. But, and this is a very large _but_, he would have to gather at least three of the highest level demons which would all have to be attacking one of you to do that."

Christi frowned, "If he was to attempt that couldn't the others of us attack them and offset their level of unrighteousness?"

Hugo shook his head, "Probably not, because each one of the higher level demons would not be affected by the lesser righteousness of your swords."

Laura shook her head. "Then they could eliminate us one by one."

Hugo nodded, "True, but you have a weapon that all the demons can't defeat, don't you Jack?"

Jack sat there and prayed for direction from Yahshua. Getting the answer, he expected, he nodded his head. "Yes, we do. Funny though, I wouldn't have expected Satan to forget that weapon so soon after Xndalius."

Hugo smiled as he thought, "This one is very wise". "That's true Jack, can you follow that concept further?"

Jack nodded, "Unfortunately, I can do just that. This whole China thing is a massive setup to give the demonic a chance to acquire the ultimate weapon, right?"

Hugo nodded his head, "Most likely, seeing that it all rose up right after Xndalius was destroyed by you with that weapon. I believe he plans to somehow force you to use that weapon to save one or more of your team and allow him to wrest control of it from you at that time. If he can't arrange it, say you don't go back, he'll be content to keep on having all the millions of Christians killed in China."

Charlie spoke up, "Which Satan has already figured out the fact the threat will make Jack go back to complete the Quest."

Jack nodded, "The only thing Satan doesn't know is what the cost will be to him to have me use that weapon in hell." He thinks I will use it to destroy the higher level demons attacking us. What if I declare the target is him, or all higher level demons, or all demons?"

Hugo was quite sober when he responded. "I have no idea of the disasters those choices would result in for the entire world. I know you won't destroy Satan, because his fate has already been set as you know from the word of God, therefore, you will not be allowed to kill him.."

Jack laughed an icy laugh, "Are you forgetting that Yahveh himself has spoken of erasing Satan and rewriting history?"

Hugo sighed, "No, I have not forgotten that, I just don't know if He will allow you to do it."

Jack said, "Let's pray and see what God has to say about my using this "ultimate" weapon."

CHAPTER THIRTY-THREE

The first word of honor and praise hadn't even reached his lips before Yahshua responded by appearing next to the team. Everyone knelt down and bowed their heads in honor to the Messiah. He said, "Rise warriors." As they stood to their feet Yahshua stepped over to Jack and placed his left hand on Jack's chest. As the Son of God looked into his eyes, Jack felt the strangest sensation, as if eternity flooded into his body. It was an enumeration of every cell in his body and a strengthening. He had felt fit, hale and hardy before but this was above those feelings like true love is above puppy love. It was wonderful! He wished he could share this feeling with Laura and everyone in the entire crossfire team.

Yahshua smiled and said, "So be it. There was a collective sigh of happiness from everyone there plus some laughing and giggles.

The Prince of Peace commented, "Your heart truly cares for others even before yourself. That is as it should be. When Lucifer causes you to use your special weapon, destroy only all demons like the ones attacking your team within ten miles. That will cripple Satan but not destroy the entire demonic realm. Then bind him immediately and let Christi discuss his, few remaining options with him. I think he'll cooperate on China and not go back on his promise."

Jack asked, "Lord, why will he keep his promise this time?"

Yahshua smiled "Because he will believe that she will end his time on this Earth if he breaks his word."

Yahshua blessed them all and faded away.

Jack prayed his grateful thanks to a God who has love for all of them.

Hugo wished them all well and disappeared himself.

Jack told Raquel to take them back and the red world reappeared around them. Their armor and swords appeared and everyone prayed for their protective field.

There was a feeling of war in that place and the group moved forward slowly. Several dozen demons charged them and were destroyed quickly. Charlie cautioned everyone to be on guard for foul play which proved prophetic when a wall several stories tall was collapsed onto the team, burying them in tons of rock and dirt. Everyone "saw" the debris moving out of their way which cleared the area around them and buried several hundred demons all around them.

That was when things got serious. A dozen large demons with capes and jeweled headbands appeared and headed toward the team. Satan showed up and laughed at them. "Now you will die like you should!"

Jack decided to end that threat immediately. He concentrated on the approaching demons and prayed for God's creative power analog. He felt the energy increase beyond comprehension and declared in a strong voice, ". **"In the name and by the authority of Yahveh God, I destroy all demons of this type within a 10-mile distance!"**

The twelve confident demons shattered into thousands of fragments and Jack spoke again. **"In the name and by the authority of Yahshua Messiah I bind Satan in cords of light so that he cannot escape nor use his powers while bound!"**

The devil was completely bound in cords of light where he stood. Jack looked at Christi. "Have fun. We'll protect you while you chat with "Old Sparky", as Mark calls him.

As Christi drew her sword of light and vectored toward the bound figure, Jack assigned the other six people and the three Angels to prevent her conversation from being interrupted.

Christi walked up to Satan and asked him if he had forgotten what they talked about earlier. She put the tip of her sword against his throat and waited for an answer.

The figure of Satan blurred and disappeared. The ropes of light faded out also. Christi double-timed it back to Jack. "We've got problems!"

Raquel suddenly transferred the entire team to the room in the third heaven. He went to seek God for an explanation of the inability to bind Satan.

Raquel returned a while later and floated near Jack. "The Most High explained events to me that will not be understandable by you at present because it takes an understanding of the operations of multiple other dimensions you do not know about. Essentially, what happened is this. Satan orchestrated the entire sequence to analyze the power used by you so that he can duplicate it for his own use. The major problem here is that he doesn't have the capability to arrange or analyze anything. Remember, he has no creative ability whatsoever."

Jack had been wondering the same thing. "So, this means the "Trifect of Si-Ogny" is setting all this up to give Satan the upper hand!"

Raquel nodded, "Except that is probably a false name because Satan lies more than he speaks the truth, even in his anger. And, one more thing. The Most High wanted this event to happen exactly as it has played out."

Jack was confused. "I don't understand. Why would God want me to use that power and let Satan's backer learn it's a secret?

A deeper voice joined in to the discussion. "Because it was a lure to expose this "backer" to God." Hugo stood there and smiled. "And it did just that. The Most High has sent the "Backer" out of our space-time continuum forever. Satan got nothing. The power you felt and the destruction of the arch demons was done by the Most High. I regret that it was your belief that was the crucial ingredient to make the "Backer" believe it was real so he could be identified and dealt with. You had to believe in your ability to use that ultimate power so that he would believe it too.

Jack didn't know if he felt embarrassed at being used as a pawn or relieved that Satan got nothing and lost his source of creativity. A wave of peace flooded over him and he heard Yahshua say, *Thank you Jack, your integrity and belief in your actually having the power is what made the devil and his backer believe the operation was real. Your reward will be great in heaven. And, the power of negative creation is real. You used it to destroy Xndalius. Understand that this operation was absolutely necessary to draw out the real villain."*

Jack wondered aloud, "Was there really a national program insisting that Christians should be killed in China?"

Hugo smiled, "There was until Christi eliminated Captain Thu Chang while you were in jail. The Quest and the mission have been successfully completed and you may return to the Sword now."

They found themselves in the meeting hall/dining room of the Sword.

Jack gave everyone, including himself and Laura, six hours to rest and then scheduled a complete team meeting. He headed toward the War Room and they ran into Mark on the way. "Welcome home Sailors." It was evident that Mark was happy to see them.

Jack hugged his best friend and asked how things were going on here while they had been away.

Mark grinned a mysterious grin and he sobered up a lot. "We need to talk."

As Jack and Laura headed to their rooms, Laura spoke quietly. "I think this is the first time I've seen Mark facing something bigger than he can handle. I have a bad feeling about this."

CHAPTER THIRTY-FOUR

Six hours later, Jack called the assembly to order. When it was quiet he stood up, "The reason for this meeting is to bring everyone on the team up to date on our latest mission."

Mark spoke up, "How is old Sparky?"

Jack grinned, "Unhappy, and he has probably elevated me to his most wanted list just behind you."

Mark whistled, "Wow, it took me several meetings with the ultimate evil to get him that mad! You did it in one pass. I congratulate you."

As the laughter calmed down, Jack described the Mission and the Quest aided by fill-in comments from the others who were on the trip.

Jack then explained the whole mission from God's angle. "God knew that Satan and the demonic was getting high-level creative help from someone not of our universe. Because this entity was super intelligent and it could remain hidden from God and Heaven. This tells me that there are many levels above us in constant conflict. Possibly on God's level, with their own universes. This is just my speculation, but it explains how they were getting away with this cooperation behind God's back."

"So, God set up an operation that seemed to give this backer an opportunity to steal an irresistible prize, the power of Negative Creation. To make this seem reasonable, He allowed Satan to put our team in a position of being destroyed or using this great power. The enemy was aware I had once before been given this power to destroy the demon Xndalius. So when I invoked this power they were ready to steal it from me. But, as soon as the villain exposed himself to steal the power, God banished him from our, and I quote the Angel Hugo, our "Space-Time Continuum". I actually never had access to the power this time. But, I believed I had it and performed as if I had it. My belief convinced this super intelligence I was going to use it when I did. God made my command actually do what would have happened if I truly had used the power."

"So, Satan lost a complete upper level of demons, at least in a ten-mile radius. He also lost his super smart backer, and he lost the one man that was attempting to rid China of Christians when Christi eliminated Thu Chang at the jail. All in all, a good ending to a major problem for everyone."

During the question and answer period, one of the SOG warriors. "General Malone, didn't the fact that God played you to achieve His goals bother you?"

"Not at all, Sergeant Heston. This whole world is nothing more than a testing ground for us. The importance of God's goals are so far above me I not only expect not to know God's aims but gladly welcome anything I can do to further them. To imply that anything the Father does "bothers" me is to imply that somehow I would believe I'm just as important as He is. I know better and trust God implicitly. If He needed me to fully believe in wishing on a star, I would because He needed me to. For anything He wants, I am grateful to Him. As you should be also."

The Sergeant smiled and gave Jack a thumbs-up sigh of agreement.

After the Q & A, Jack asked if there was any new business that the entire team needed to be involved in. Mark Connelly stood up. "The general meeting is over with and most of you can return to duty. I would like the Core Team to remain."

After the core team moved together, Mark looked all of them one-by-one and ended with looking at Jack and Laura. "I have been given a warning by the Angel Caleb that we need to discuss."

Mark sighed, "I'm concerned that our time with China is not over, but only beginning. It seems that Satan is not pleased with the results of your trip to China and has decided to show that fact by terrorizing all of the Far East, starting with Beijing. According to Caleb, the demonic has over three million demons, with bodies, already in our dimension so he doesn't have to seek God's approval to bring them in. They were somewhat already "Grandfathered in" before the new rules and Satan plans to use them all in this effort."

The Father in Heaven created our team, along with eleven more like us, to counter Satan's use of embodied demons to create fear and chaos in this world. So, it falls on us to stop this. It reminds me of our trip to Russia, only multiplied by a thousand. So, ideas, comments, procedures, tactics, etc.?"

Jack had listened to the challenge and had been praying that God would reveal how they, all thirty-five of them could battle millions of demons and win.

Laura spoke up. "What about the millions of Angels in Heaven, the Heavenly Host? Can they assist use in this matter?"

Jack spoke out, "Raquel!"

The Archangel appeared in his Crossfire Team uniform and sat down next to Jack. "We can help. There are also millions of other duties and emergencies that the Heavenly Host has to handle on a daily basis. So, the bulk of Angels are not free just for this one problem. But, depending on the load, we can muster a goodly amount of swords at any one time. How are you going to meet this challenge?"

Jack smiled, "We're in the planning stages right now. Can you stay and keep us on course?"

Raquel look introspective for a minute. "Yes, I can assist you for a while."

The planning went on until the late evening. At the conclusion it was agreed that their entire effort would hinge on the cooperation of the Chinese Government and that would require the assistance of the President of China."

CHAPTER THIRTY-FIVE

Mark sighed (again). "We've had pretty poor results with convincing Atheistic leaders to cooperate with us in the past. Russia invited us in to help them and then tried to kill us as a reward the first time. The second time we convinced the Russian President but ended up getting him removed from office and terminated. The Chinese Security Premier rejected our offers, and I don't think the British or the French like us either. Any insights on how we can get the backing of the Chinese Government to stop the demonic attacks on their country?"

Jack had been alternately thinking about that and praying for more guidance in the matter. As he started to pray to Yahshua again he had that feeling of shifting that accompanied their trips to Heaven in the past. He opened his eyes to see a great deal of things going on that made no sense to him. He looked around and didn't see anyone he recognized. He started to walk in one direction and the whole area around him seemed to realign by rotating to his right. Now he was facing an avenue that had been to his left a second ago.

Obviously he was supposed to go this way. So he walked along trying to interpret what he saw happening near him. At one place people were working on something that sort of looked like a table with several tops one above the other. But, the tops were constantly in motion or flux and would disappear out of sight only to reappear later. The people working, or whatever they were doing, would take something off of one of the table tops and do something with the object in their hands and then move it to one side where it disappeared.

In another place he watched two people moving their arms and hands. As they moved, colors would appear in the air behind their fingers and remained as the hands moved on. Soon they had created a shape with beautiful curves and shadings. As they continued to create additional shapes and forms the overall structure grew in size and began moving around. It reminded Jack of something but he couldn't remember what it was. Just that the overall creation reminded him of something.

He eventually came to a building of marvelous beauty and a door opened in the closest side. He entered the building and felt great peace in his soul. He knew he was going where he should be going and then he saw the Angel Rose.

She waved him over to a comfortable-looking couch and had him sit down. He still felt the peace within him as she smiled at him. "Welcome Jack Malone. The Most High wanted you to see a little bit of this part of the third Heaven before He answers your prayer for direction. How are you?"

Jack drew in a deep breath and smiled back at the lovely Angel. "I'm fine Rose. I must admit that I didn't understand any of what was happening out there. What were the people, or Angels, doing creating colorful shapes?"

Rose nodded her head. "They were creating cloud formations and sunset hues that you've seen in the skies of Earth. There are many Angels involved in that process."

The connection snapped into place for Jack. "Oh, I see."

The voice of God filled Jack's mind. *"Jack, I wanted you to get a slight taste of your Heavenly home before sending you back to the battle. My instruction to you and the others of your team are this, Satan does not have to seek my approval to bring the demons into the Earth dimension. While that is true, he still must ask permission to use those forces against the population of my children on Earth. Your Watcher-on-the-Wall, Carol, will be able to advise you as to when and where Satan will deploy his forces and what they are trying to do. You can then plan on how to stop them from reaching their goals. Leave the Government of China alone because they will soon realize the nature of the demonic forces and your defense of their country and its people. They will then understand and provide all the help they can to support your team. Have Raquel use the Heavenly Host as needed to prevent Satan from simply overwhelming your team or your resources. The battles will be fierce but this has to happen for all scripture to be true. Go with my power in everything you do and all necessary powers will be available to you as you need them. I will be with you also."*

Jack was back in the War Room on the Sword and knew he had been given the answers he needed. He looked over at Laura and she smiled at him. "You're glowing again." she said.

Jack related what God had told him and saw the true understanding on the other team member's faces.

Mark then recapped their plan to counter Satan's terror program. "We will set up our base in Beijing and set up teams of twos. That means we can react to seventeen incursions at the same time. Yes, Satan can field a lot more than that at once, but we will have the Angels of the Heavenly Host to help us. I, personally, feel that the Demonic will start with only a few operations to instill fear in the general population and then build on that. Each of us has our armor and swords and if the press of demons gets too great, we can use the protective energy field. We now know we can pray for the field and it doesn't require a physical generator to make it available. God will decide if we need to use the field or not."

The Core Team broke up and went to make preparations to fight this latest battle.

Jack had been quiet for a while and Mark studied him. "Okay buddy, what is that agile mind of yours cooking up? I've seen the signs before. You've got a new concept or problem. Tell me what it is before I have to make a real fuss."

Jack grinned, "As was said before, this is a lot like the Russian campaign and you triggered a chain of thought with your comment about our "reacting" to the devil's incursions. Remember that Satan isn't creative, this will probably be run exactly like the one in Russia because it's a repeat of that operation. But, God gave us creative powers, so, let's think outside the box and get creative. What if we split our forces and leave the majority here to prevent these incursions from running wild? Then, a select group goes on the offensive in Satan's domain and reverses the program by attacking his critical operations and wounding his capabilities?"

Mark blinked twice and smiled. "I like it! We could give old sparky all kinds of grief to distract him from the China campaign! Also, we could seriously hinder his end-times efforts too. All right, who goes to war and who goes to hell?"

Jack held up his hand, "Hold on partner, let's get a Heavenly reaction to this concept first."

Mark agreed, both he and Jack said together, "Raquel".

CHAPTER THIRTY-SIX

The Archangel appeared in his warrior angel apparel and His sword out with demon stain running off of it. He raised an eyebrow at the looks on the faces of the two men. "How can I be of service? I see skull-duggery at work in both of your countenances."

Mark smiled, "If you can pause in your important business, we'd like to solicit your opinion on a business deal we are contemplating. That is, if you have a little time to spend with us."

Raquel sheathed his sword and nodded his head. "Certainly I can give you my time here. This other business won't miss me while I'm gone. What fiendish plan are you concocting to make Satan go insane this time?"

Jack grinned at the Angel, "Funny you should mention that, because that is exactly what we want your opinion on." Jack explained their defense of China and their design to attack Satan's operations in the demonic dimension at the same time to force Satan to defend his turf and lessen the attack on the human dimension.

Raquel shook his head, "I actually expected something like this after your victory against Satan in hell, Jack. I am not creative either, but I knew when you got together with Satan's biggest pain in his existence, Mark Connelly, you two would definitely want to go back there together to eliminate any link Satan has with rational thought."

Mark tipped his head to one side. "Do you think our plan could be approved by Heaven?"

Raquel sighed, "I considered this possibility and brought this idea up to the Most High. I believe He not only approves of it, but is pleased to be behind a plan of this type completely. Which then makes me wonder if this could be an another complex plan by Satan to get you both into his grasp."

Mark shook his head, "By now you'd think he would know better."

Jack asked, "Raquel, can you come up with a list of high-priority targets in that domain for us to take down?"

Raquel asked, "When do you plan to start this "attack" on the demonic?"

Mark grinned, "Right after the first demonic attack in China. We don't want to be the aggressors, now do we?" Mark realized he was quoting the same thing Jack had said about the ten Russian fighter jets.

Raquel nodded his head. "I'll have a list and locations by then. Oh, by the way, Jack's trip has created a new drive in several Angels. You'll have the same three Angel team with you this time also." Raquel was drawing his sword as he faded out of sight.

Mark looked at Jack, "You think that is God's way of keeping tabs on our activities?"

Jack shook his head, "No, these are the messengers and warriors of the Most High. He already knows the end from the beginning for everything. I think we've created a new breed of Angels, excitement seekers."

Mark nodded, "Okay, who is going with us?

Jack thought about that. "Our wives for sure, Christi, Charlie and Linda Wu, Ariella, and Elon."

Mark nodded, "Okay, then David and Alexis can run the defense with Ethan Reaper to coordinate all of our activities."

Jack concurred and sent orders to everyone.

The Sword had again moved close to China and the defense teams were airlifted to the outskirts of the Major city of Beijing. With the help of Han Le they set up a base of operations in an abandoned and secluded warehouse. David set up the teams in two-person sets to respond to the demonic incursions as Carol identified the targets. Then they waited.

Jack had been praying for God's protection from demonic knowledge so that the raiders would not be expected. The away team met and discussed logistics and tactics. After that talk, Elon and Ariella decided to stay with the defensive team and allow two more experienced warriors tackle the assault on hell.

Jack recalled Two of the SOG warriors sent to the defense team and filled their spots on that team with Elon and Ariella.

Captain Randell Eckhart, and Lieutenant Eva Stephenson had been with the team since the inception of the Special Operations Group and were very capable sword bearers. Jack welcomed them to the away team. "Randy, Eva, I appreciate your willingness to join with us, somewhat critically, focused people of the Core Team in our assault on the demonic realm.

Both new team members shook hands all around and greeted the others they had shared battles with over the last years.

Mark filled them in on the planned operation and made sure they could pray in their "force generator fields" which they decided to now call "defensive field" because the force generator had always been God's anyway.

The first assault on Beijing happened at five o'clock Friday afternoon at a major fish seller storefront. Warned by Carol Two two-person teams and twelve Angels were in place and stopped the attack in the street outside the market. David, Alexis, and two SOG warriors met the twenty demons exiting the rift and did battle. The twelve Angels joined in and the battle was over in less than fifteen minutes. No causalities or losses on the good guy's side and no survivors on the demonic side. The rift faded out and disappeared. The test battle ended up 0 to 1 for Satan. As they headed back to their base, David said, "Now that they know how we will respond, this is where the real battle begins."

Jack, Mark, and the others of the away team made their first attack into the demonic at that time. Raquel had shown them where they were going to strike and what they were going to destroy.

Sarah frowned and stared at Mark. She then summed up their target. "Let me see if I've got this straight. The nine of us, along with a couple of Archangels and the Angel Rose, are going into the demonic realm we call hell. We are going to attack the operations control center for demonic oppression and terrorization of children in our world. An area with roughly two thousand demons and Arch demons, all of who really don't like us. And, it is a Mark Connelly type raid that leaves no demons alive and culminates with us burning the whole place down. Then we need to stay alive long enough to exfiltrate to our dimension. That pretty well covers it, right?

Mark nodded, "Yeah, that's about it. But you left out the parts where we have a ton of demon killing ammo, including some new explosives that will do the clearing for us, and that we all get to use our defensive fields because we're so badly out-numbered in that realm. That means we each only have to take out roughly 167 demons each. We've done that in a normal day here on Earth."

Sarah smiled, "Oh well, if you put it like that, it doesn't sound too bad."

Randy and Eva looked at each other and smiled.

Jack looked around at everyone and told Raquel to take them on their trip.

CHAPTER THIRTY-SEVEN

The brightly lighted space in the Assembly Room on the Sword was suddenly replaced by the red-lit gloom of the Demonic domain. They were spotted immediately by several demons who came charging toward them. The Angels Caleb and Rose met the demons' half-way between the team and the outer limits of their target area.

Caleb dispatched the first two demons with two swings of his golden sword. Rose decapitated the third demon with a feint that put the demon at a disadvantage. The rest of the team caught up with them and congratulated them on their efficiency.

Randy asked Mark why the other demons weren't attacking them. Mark shook his head, "Because they're lower level demons and they're dumb. Instead of alerting the others they just tried to resolve the problem by themselves. Don't worry, once a higher-level command demon discovers we're here, we'll get really busy."

Charlie and Sarah were scoping out various area of incomprehensible labor. Finding the apparent center of activity for this section, they selected the route to get them there in the least amount of time. Raquel agreed that was the most critical spot. Jack set the order of advancement for the nine humans. He knew the Angels would pick the best formation as they wished.

He set Mark as lead, then Charlie and himself behind and to each side of Mark Then a row with Sarah, Eva, and Laura side by side. Next came Linda Wu behind Laura and Randy behind Sarah. Christi came last in the tail position. Christi knew the battle could easily switch making her the lead at any time.

As the middle person, Eva was charged with using her Bullpup-style rifle with a box magazine holding 300 rounds of the special Holy caseless ammo. She was a specialist in marksmanship and sniping. Her job, in this case, was not direct sword fighting, at least to begin with. She would continue to take out leaders or any other target of opportunity while those around her were involved in hand-to-claw fighting.

As the group moved forward, the demons all started charging away from them to the left of the team's approach. Jack could see Raquel, Caleb, and Rose chopping down demons right and left and smashing their way into the target on that side. The humans had to admire the huge diversion that created.

As they waited for the demons to clear their path Ava asked Mark, "I understand that the demons that we fight in our dimension have been given a body so as to have a physical presence. But, all the demons here already have bodies, where do they come from? These bodies here?"

Mark nodded, "I understand how that can be confusing. The difference is that here, in the demonic realm, these are their normal bodies which cannot exist in our realm. They would be invisible in our realm and the demons would function simply as the invisible, immaterial evil spirits they are. When we battle them here and cut them down their spirit being is condemned to the pit just like when we kill their borrowed real bodies in our dimension. Satan wants to spread fear of the demonic in our realm and the demons need a physical presence to do that. If you're still not sure, talk to one of the Angels. It has to do with the rules governing the eleven different dimensions."

Ava grinned, "That's all right, I get the drift." She brushed her Auburn hair back with her left hand."It doesn't matter in the long run, just kill them no matter what dimension we're in at the time."

Mark smiled, "Good advice, Lieutenant."

Jack waved everyone forward and they double timed it into the room, building, area, whatever it was and attacked the demons there with a vengeance. The ammo with the essence of God in the tip killed every demon it hit and soon there were no more demons to be seen. Jack took a deep breath and called the team together. "Good job. I assume we are about the get a visit from a major upper-level demon or Satan himself. Our weapons will probably not kill the more powerful demons due to their greater unrighteous. Let me handle those. If Satan shows up, do not try to kill him. That's not our job. He figures in the Biblical End Times and his fate is already determined."

Jack looked around and shrugged his shoulders. "In the meantime, let's destroy the rest of this operation." They continued to kill any demons they encountered. They set explosives to anything they could find that looked important or that the Angels pointed out to them. After several hours of this mayhem they were resting when a high level demon appeared. It tried to kill them but was stymied by the defensive field. Their weapons couldn't overcome the large demon's unrighteousness either. Realizing that the standoff wouldn't last forever, Jack held up his hand and stopped the combat. He approached the large demon and spoke to it. "Tell Satan that we will be destroying his entire kingdom one piece at a time unless he cancels the attacks on our Asian brothers and sisters in China."

The big demon studied Jack for a bit and subtly tested the strength of the defensive field. Finding no weaknesses, it spoke back. "I don't usually speak to human scum like you since you cannot kill me. But, since I can't destroy you either, I will make an exception in your case. My master says if you don't stop annoying him he will double the attacks in Asia immediately."

Jack had expected as much and was about to order the resumption of their attack when Mark stepped past Jack and got, literally, in the demon's face. "Tell Old Sparky, that Mark Connelly says, "Since you are so stupid that you would increase your attacks to threaten us, and through us, the one that sent us, I will see your threat and double the wager. Instead of this time-consuming house-to-house combat we will use a more effective method, observe."

Mark lifted a small control unit and pushed the red button on it. Ten feet away, behind the team, a fifty-kiloton, backpack nuclear weapon detonated and when the blinding white glare dissipated, the area for a mile in all directions was totally obliterated. The damage for another mile in diameter was in rubble or on fire or both.

The demon had been shielded, in large, by the defensive fields of the team between the bomb and itself, but not completely. It had lost all of its apparel, some of its skin, and had large black blisters over a goodly part of its already hideous body. It was shaking uncontrollably and possibly blind.

Mark smiled, "Oh, by the way, that was one of the smallest bombs we have in our arsenal and from the looks of you, I wouldn't bet on your concept that we can't kill you. Now be a good little demon and scurry back to your master and see if he wants to continue to test us."

As the huge, stinky, and slightly smoking demon faded out of sight, Jack turned to Mark. "Now, that's what I call an effective demonstration. Though, in the future I will ask you to give me a heads-up when you're going to detonate a nuclear weapon during our negotiations."

Mark looked at Jack, "What? You're going to tell me you didn't see that coming?"

Jack looked back to where the demon had stood, "No, and I'm pretty sure Satan's henchman didn't see it coming either."

Things were still exploding or falling apart around them as far as the eye could see when Jack suggested that Raquel take them home.

Back on the Sword the team did their reports and cleaned up before meeting to recap their mission. Laura slapped Mark on the back hard enough to jar him. "I told Jack that I wanted him to *tell* me what it was like to be at the center of a nuclear explosion after you two did it with that submarine off of our island base. I also told him I *never* wanted to do it myself! I appreciate your demonstrating it so effectively, but, please, don't do that again while I'm around, it still scares me, okay?"

Mark nodded, "Sorry, I'll make sure that it doesn't happen again while you're there."

Sarah smiled, "I don't know, I rather liked it. It's not something everyone gets to see. And live to tell about it."

CHAPTER THIRTY-EIGHT

Satan stood before Yahshua and complained, "It is unfair that this disgusting group of humans can have free access to my domain to destroy what they want and I can't touch them!

The Son of God studied the rebellious Angel and asked him, *"Yet, you feel it is fair for you to have access to their realm and kill, steal, and destroy anyone or anything you desire? Do you not have millions of demons? Are not each of them more powerful than the strongest human? The Crossfire team is less than fifty souls and because my Father gives them tools to even the odds against your millions you find it unfair? Accept it, and don't whine, there is little time left before your end."*

The devil shook his head, "No, I will not accept it. I demand by the rules of heaven that I be given an equal battlefield with the Crossfire Team in my dimension! It is my right!"

Yahshua sighed, *"What is it you want, Satan?"*

"I want the Crossfire Team's protective shields not to work in my realm! Is that too much to ask?"

Yahshua thought for a bit. *"It shall be as you desire. Now, be gone before I change my mind."*

The devil grinned and disappeared.

Back on Earth, in the War Room on the Sword, the Core Team was discussing their progress against Satan when Raquel appeared among them.

Jack greeted the Archangel and asked him if he wanted to join the discussion. Raquel was in his Angel attire and he declined the offer. "I bring you news from the Most High. Now hear the word of the Lord. *"Warriors of the Crossfire Team, your enemy has petitioned Me to give him a fair chance against your team in his realm. To "level" the battlefield I agreed to not allow your team the use of the protection field while in the demonic domain. This exposes each of your warriors, which take the battle against Satan, in his realm, to the maiming and lethal forces he can bring against you. While this may seem an unfair advantage against you because of your few numbers, it is in the quest for righteousness that it must be met. Do not be discouraged for I will be with you and if you resist the devil, he will flee.*

Raquel frowned, "Of course this applies to the Angels also. We can't fight off the hundreds of demons that Satan can bring against us in the demonic realm. But, if you plan to continue this battle with Satan we will go with you and fight as long as we can stand." The Archangel faded out of sight.

Mark looked at the concerned faces around him. "Come on people! Don't look so glum. We can still beat Old Sparky in his own back yard. When you can't go head-to-head with an opponent, you resort to guerrilla tactics. We can keep our promise to Satan by quick raids. Arrive, strike, be gone before they can mount an assault against us. It will work. especially against the Devil. We'll just use his own tactics against him. For instance, how much better will it be for us when we're done we just escape back into our dimension than trying to exfiltrate?

Christi said, "True, but don't we get listed on the matrix too? Won't the devil know where, when, and why we're entering his domain?"

Jack grunted, "Yeah, there is that little problem."

Mark was thinking quickly. "That could be a problem, but I think there is a way around that."

David laughed, "Have you seen what God does to the devil when he cheats on the Matrix?"

Mark smiled, "Wait and see, O' Wise One."

Mark enlisted Jack, David, Ethan, and Charlie to help him plan the next three sets of attacks if Satan continued demonic attacks on China. The devil, emboldened by eliminating the defensive fields, actually doubled the next attacks in Beijing.

Laura asked Jack, "Do you believe Mark's new style of attacks will work and not leave the team facing insurmountable counter attacks?"

Jack smiled, "Mark is one smart military planner. He has a really outrageous concept and I do think it will achieve all four goals. It will keep us safe, it will damage Satan's operations, it should totally confuse the demonic hierarchy, and it should drive Satan to new levels of insanity."

She smiled, "Does it involve nuclear weapons?"

Jack nodded, "Occasionally, depending on Satan's reactions to our counter-attacks. I, for one, am very glad Mark Connelly is on our side."

Laura grimaced, "Have you checked with God on these new types of attacks?"

"Yes, I have, and as a team, we have gotten God's approval of everything we're going to do. I will make a million-dollar wager that Satan will stop his attacks on China within two weeks and ask God to call us off! Which of course we'll do as long as he doesn't renege on his agreement to stop his attacks. He definitely doesn't want to suffer Mark's Plan B."

She pursed her lips. "This I've got to see."

Upon commencement of the new, enlarged attacks on Beijing, Mark took Jack, Sarah, Christi, Charlie and Linda Wu, Ariella, and Elon along with their trio of Angels on the retaliatory attack. Having given precise instructions to Carol and praying for Heavenly Permission, they appeared near their second target and attracted the attention of many demons. They defeated fifty or so demons and then withdrew into a structure of sorts and continued to snipe at any demons they saw.

Raquel had been watching the massing of demonic hordes and upper level leaders. When there were literally thousands of demons surrounding the structure, the signal to attack was given and rewards offered for each human or Heavenly Angel killed. There would be no way the humans could escape because the mass of demons had forged an ironclad sphere of demonic energy around the structure that a hundred Archangels couldn't penetrate to escape back to the human realm.

Hundreds of demons attacked from each side and from above as well. There were demons in the sewers and underground to ensure the hated humans and Angels couldn't crawl out that way. The humans had barricaded the entrances but the demons could smell them and hear their voices and a real frenzy took over the attack. They could pay back the Crossfire Team for all the defeats at their hands!

Mark looked at Raquel. "They've got the building surrounded?"

Raquel nodded.

They've completely blocked us from getting back to our dimension, you're sure?

Again the nod.

"And the eight of us are facing ten thousand demons and upper level demon masters?"

Raquel solemnly said, "There is no hope of us escaping no matter what we do."

Mark listened to the insane howling and inhuman screams and looked at the others. "Well then, I guess it's time." He pushed the button.

The flash of the two kiloton nuclear weapon was silent in its power and purity. For about two milliseconds. Then with a noise that could not be measured, the entire structure and all the demons, not to mention everything else within two miles of ground zero was reduced to elemental fragments. The heat and light burned, or charred anything within another mile. The traditional "mushroom" cloud was torn to pieces by the tornadic winds created by the blast. The entire sector of the demonic realm disappeared in less than ten minutes.

Satan was furious and gleeful in equal amounts because his kingdom had lost eight vital operations that couldn't be replaced, but he was finally rid of the main players of the Crossfire Team. He didn't give a hoot about the thousands of demons lost to him. He had millions more to use. He was finally rid of Mark Connelly! Oh, how good that felt. He had seen the woman Christi and even the mighty Jack Malone with Mark. Well, they won't be missed either. He decided to take a break and consider how much their loss would hurt Yahshua. It was his fault! He caved and denied them their precious defensive fields. Without them, they couldn't live through their own explosion. HAH!

CHAPTER THIRTY-NINE

David Zahavy looked at Laura in the War Room on the Sword. "Well, they certainly knew the odds going in, didn't they?"

Laura nodded her head, "Yes they did. Have we heard what the news is from the demonic realm?"

David nodded, "According to Caleb, the explosion destroyed all of an entire sector of hell along with all of the demons and demonic overlords in the area. Estimates range between fifteen thousand to forty thousand demons perished in the blast. I have no idea what radiation does to demons, probably just makes them uglier."

Alexis looked at her husband, "Is that possible?"

David shook his head. "Caleb also told me that Satan is celebrating the demise of the leaders of the Team and apparently counts his losses as acceptable to simply get rid of Mark."

Laura laughed, "He is going to regret crowing over Mark's death."

Mark smiled, "You think he'll be upset to find out that we weren't there when the bomb went off?"

Sarah also laughed, "Mark had the devil totally figured out. We planted the decoys and had Raquel translate us back here before Satan even knew we were there. By the time they sealed the place to prevent our getting out that way it was way too late. We listened to the attack and when Raquel told us it was time, Mark detonated the bomb. We accomplished our mission and then some."

Mark looked Raquel, "How can I send Satan an email or a post card and warn him not to continue his attacks? Because the next time we respond it will be worse than it was this time"

Raquel smiled, "I have just told the Most High and He has relayed your message."

Mark chuckled, "I wish I could have seen his reaction. It would have been interesting."

Raquel grinned, "I think I heard his scream of frustration from here. What are you going to do to top this if he doesn't stop the China attacks?"

"I'm going to scorch his tail feathers really well. Can you find out what his response is going to be to this challenge before he actually implements it?"

The Archangel thought for a few seconds, "I believe his answer is going to be a really massive attack on China about this time tomorrow."

Jack raised an eyebrow. "That was really quick. How do you know what his answer is already?"

Raquel shrugged, "It is actually quite easy. By comparing information from both the eighth and thirty-seventh dimensions I can see his answer now. Remember, time only constrains your race on your world."

Jack blinked, "The eighth and the thirty-seventh dimensions? I thought there were only eleven dimensions."

Raquel smiled. "There are actually an infinite number of dimensions."

Mark grinned, "Okay then, can you tell me which sector is the most precious to the devil?"

The Archangel stared at Mark, "Yes I can. Are you going to use another nuclear bomb?"

Mark shook his head, "Not this time. He'll be expecting that and I really want to disappoint him this time. If we do it right, it'll be a lot worse than a nuke for him."

Raquel laughed, "Mark Connelly, I am very glad you are on our side."

Sarah's eyes twinkled, "What are you planning this time dear husband?"

Mark looked back at her, "Shock and Awe my wife, just pure Shock and Awe."

Mark and David worked out a human dimension defense against the expected demonic attacks in China and preset the responders and Angelic backups.

Mark retired to his office in his suite of rooms and made three phone calls. He sat back and reviewed his plan and smiled.

As the clock ran down on their window of opportunity Mark and Jack huddled and prayed with Raquel and Caleb and then he used his computer. At precisely the right time he typed "NOW". Both Angels and Mark disappeared and then reappeared in the demonic dimension. Spread out before them was a large sector of tall hills and deep crevasses with many structures or possibly buildings throughout the area. All at once there were terrible noises and very loud creaking sounds and a massive shaking of the whole terrain. All of the structures and then the surrounding hills collapsed into ruin and debris. With an even louder ripping sound part of the sky or ceiling disintegrated and fell down to join the piles of rubble and blindingly bright light flooded into the stygian gloom and lit up the destruction.

Mark touched Raquel's arm and they found themselves back on the Sword. The silence was a shocking difference from the tremendous crashing and rumbling of the demonic realm they just left.

Jack thanked the Angels and they disappeared. Mark took out the micro video camera he'd used at the destruction site and reviewed the coverage. He then loaded it up to the ship's website. Walking down to the War Room he went to his seat and sat down. Christi asked, "When do we attack the demonic again?"

Mark looked at the beautiful young woman. "Hopefully never. I took care of this raid myself with some Heavenly help. He typed in a command on his console and noted, "This is the most precious sector in the demonic realm that Satan has. Watch this."

Everyone sat in actual shock and awe as they watched the total destruction of the landscape and the final wave of light washing over the rubble.

Jack looked at Mark, "Please tell us how you were able to make a HARP attack work in hell."

Mark nodded, "Well, the actual HARP attack was aimed at a desolate area of desert in the American Southwest. The Father allowed Raquel and Caleb to redirect the power into the demonic kingdom at those coordinates. Pretty effective, don't you think? The collapse of the ceiling or sky wasn't in the plan but, it was like the cherry on top of the ice cream."

Jack just started to chuckle. "I'd pay a lot to see Satan's reaction to this little action. His favorite sector? Oh Yeah, He is going to be one very unhappy demon. I think we'd better pray for Mark's protection as well as that of the whole Team from retribution by Satan."

They prayed and thanked God in His Son's name for complete protection for everyone on the world-wide Crossfire Team and especially for Mark and Sarah.

Later that day, Raquel appeared in the War Room and pointed to both Jack and Mark. "We need to talk."

The two men and Raquel disappeared. They appeared on a pleasant, sun-lit porch somewhere in Israel. Everyone sat down in chairs around a pretty tiled table. Raquel looked at Mark, "I have nominated you for the person of the century. Without a doubt you deserve the title. No one, man, woman, nor Angel has affected the relationships between Heaven, Hell, and the Human world as much as you."

Mark tipped his head to one side. "What has happened?"

"In the courts of Heaven, Satan has demanded your head on a platter to be delivered to him by God. He was so mad that he wouldn't listen to any argument by Yahshua or anyone else. He is so incensed by the destruction of the latest sector of his realm he has stopped all end-times cooperation with Heaven. He guaranteed that all prophesy will not come true if he has anything to do with it."

Jack asked, "How did God receive these threats?"

"He told Satan to return to his domain and rethink what he is demanding. Your actions were approved by Him and were a just reward for the continued attacks in China against Heaven's commands to cease them.

Satan left the courts completely unsatisfied and even madder than when he arrived. He is complaining that what he is doing is what God gave him a heart to do and what you are doing is not permitted by the covenant he has with God."

Mark nodded, "Everybody knows the devil is a liar and the truth is not in him. What are we doing here? This was not one of the possible outcomes we expected from that strike. Does God want me to apologize?"

The Archangel actually blinked, "

"Oh No! The Most High told you that what you planned to do, which was exactly what you did, was acceptable and correct. He does not make mistakes or need to rethink what He said to do. He sent me here as a Heavenly witness and protector as your prayers requested."

Mark said, "Oh, all right then. Exactly what did Old Sparky do when God gave him my message?"

You could see the mighty Archangel trying to suppress a grin and losing his battle. He laughed so loud and long, it was contagious and both Jack and Mark joined him until the tears were running freely. Even after they finally settled down, Raquel kept smiling, but he bordered on tears of laughter again.

Breathing deeply, he finally described in some detail the events as he knew them. "When the Most High gave Satan the message. According to a witness, who was suddenly in great fear for his life, the devil sat there with an extremely unheard of icy calm. Speak about waiting for the dam to break, nothing and nobody moved, unwilling to draw attention to themselves Finally, Satan stood up and walked purposely out of the room and summoned the three surviving second level demons involved in the counter attack on what they thought was you and your team. The witness was able to describe in gory detail the torture Satan meted out to them. Their broken and lifeless bodies hadn't even fallen to the ground before the devil went on a killing spree worse than any anyone had ever seen before."

"As he killed each demon he kept mumbling, "Take that Mark Connelly!", or "How do you like that Mark!". Eventually he got past that stage he started ordering many thousands of demons to attack, you, your wife, Jack and Laura, Me, Rose and Caleb, or any Angel they found. He was literally moving all hell to extract violent revenge on you. Then he did an about-face and cancelled all those plans and sought the Most High to give him you or your dead body. When the Most High refused him, he returned to the rubble that had been his mighty castle of torture and sat there scheming. The witness said he sat there so long in thought with his head on his hand that he looked just like Rodin's sculpture of "The Thinker". Then he grinned and disappeared. I am sure he has devised an extremely gruesome fate for any and all of you. According to Hugo, never has Satan been so focused before. Ergo, that is why I am here.

Mark had been thinking and praying. "Good, then I have accomplished my mission. I have taken his attention off of the Chinese and other Earthbound followers of Yahshua and put it squarely on me and the team. I assume the Most High will allow us to utilize the protection field anywhere other than the demonic domain?"

Raquel laughed again. "Allow? No, He commands you and the other team members to use them constantly for the foreseeable future. That includes the team and family members not with you for everyone. The Most High would command Satan to leave all of you alone, but He knows that old snake would not heed him, especially with time so short."

"All in all, you and the Crossfire Team are the most talked about group in the Universe right now. If Heaven had a Facebook or Twitter you would have zillions of followers. Which only adds fuel to the fire for Satan."

CHAPTER FORTY

Carol Moffet was a cute younger woman who had visited the Crossfire Team when they were in their original fortress in Colorado, USA. She had arrived to give the Team vital information on Thermal Energy Generation, her field of expertise. Events followed that had brought her into the Team as their "Watcher on the Wall" which refers to the earlier days of groups like the Hebrews who kept a man on the highest parapet who could see in all direction and warn the soldiers of threats headed toward their city.

Carol Moffet had grown up living a protected childhood and being home schooled K-12 by loving and considerate parents in Yuma, Arizona. She secretly felt she had occasional wild times, which would have been considered as boring by most public school graduates, and she felt she was a bit of a rebel. After finishing the high school grades, she found that she excelled at computers and physics and had gone to a private school for her college work. She was rated as one of the best software engineers in the world of geophysical research by the time she graduated with honors.

She had taken a premier position with the new "GTherm Corporation" and quickly established herself as a very young but brilliant theoretical physicist in the new world of Geothermal Power. She easily assumed the position of leadership in her design group and was respected by everyone despite her young age of twenty-two.

A terrorist organization attacked her place of business and the Crossfire Team had saved her life and eliminated the attackers. While in Colorado she witnessed the kidnapping of Jack and Laura Malone by a demon and helped pray for their healing when they were rescued. God took the Core Team and Carol to Heaven to explain in eleven dimensions why the event had to happen. After that, He anointed Carol to read and interpret the "Matrix" in an alternative dimension. On the Matrix, which she could visit in the spirit, were all the requests made to God, including all those of the demonic world. She was limited to only those events affecting the Team. After several years of Heavenly training by Hugo, the training Angel, she was very good at her calling. God had also given her two symbols that showed when she was doing her duty. A diamond-shaped jewel on her forehead and one on her throat. When she was "away" these symbols glowed with the essence of God.

Carol called Mark to tell him that there were no more indications on the matrix concerning demonic attacks on China. Mark thanked her and notified the rest of the team.

Another young woman had been hired onto the team when Christi Steele had joined them. Her name was Rachel Reynolds.

Rachel had been an aspiring actress in Denver Colorado and a good friend of Christi when God brought Christi to join the team. Rachel was gifted in the areas of acting and other activities that resulted in her joining the team and training as a spy to assist Carol Moffet after she was trained by the Israeli Kidon. Christi shipped out when the team moved to the Sword as their new, mobile base.

Christi got a call from Rachel and they talked for a bit. Rachel told her about her training and her first assignment. Then she got to current events. "Christi! Two days ago I was suddenly taken up to Heaven and spent four days there. An Angel named Hugo trained about twenty people, including not only me but your Mom and Stepdad in the use and rules of a "Defensive Field". Hugo told us we need to pray for and use these fields for the foreseeable future because Satan will try to hurt us if we don't have them on. Boy, this is great! Nothing, and I mean nothing, can hurt me. Isn't that great?"

Christi smiled to herself and thought, "If she only knew." Then she realized Rachel was part of the team and this was a secure line per Ethan Reaper, "Listen Rachel, I've been using the field on an as-needed basis for over a year already. I'll give you an idea of how good these things are. A week ago I was using the field when a Backpack Nuclear Weapon was detonated less than eight feet from me. I didn't even feel a breeze, but everything around me for about a half mile was utterly destroyed. Remember Jack and Laura, David, and Mark and Sarah? They were using their fields and they all jumped out of an aircraft at forty thousand feet altitude, without parachutes! They demolished an entire terrorist base when they hit. Best of all, God had me call Satan to account and he couldn't hurt me. I'll have to tell you about some of the other things too. Look babe, I'm glad to hear from you, stay safe, I have to go. Bye."

Now that the mini war over China was done, at least for now, Jack got back to tending to other Team business. He made a call to Captain Robert Maxwell. Rob was one of the leaders of the Crossfire Air Force and Research division. He had also recently joined the Team as an anointed Swordsman due to his encounter with demons trying to kill him while flying air cover for a battle with the Team.

Rob took the call and asked if he could see Jack for a new weapons meeting. Jack set up the meeting and praying to the Father about the meeting he was led to include Mark and Hugh Kelly, the Executive Officer of the Sword itself.

When Rob got there he greeted all three men and got right into it. "Gentlemen, I've told you on previous occasions that the group of engineers and developers, both here on the Sword and in our base in the South Pacific are a really creative bunch and we try to give them free reign to develop whatever they feel will be needed and make it slightly ahead of leading edge technology. Our primary function is the Crossfire Team and their needs. Right? Well, I believe they may have outdone all their previous efforts this time. And, the amazing thing is they did it in a field pretty much unrelated to aviation."

That got everyone's attention. Jack asked, "What have they come up with this time?"

Rob keyed a small control in his hand and out of the tiny package a light threw a vivid three-dimensional photograph on the wall of the conference room. Displayed was a vehicle that somewhat echoed the ultra-modern aircraft the R&D group had produced such as the "Fragment", Ghost, and the "Formidable".

It was a somewhat sleeker shape of indeterminate size since there was nothing else in the image to compare it to.

Rob spoke quietly. "Gentlemen, what you're looking at is a next generation NAV or Naval Attack Vehicle. This beauty is seventy-seven feet long and twenty-eight feet wide. It stands twenty feet high and weighs twelve tons. It can be operated by one person, if need be, but normally requires a crew of three. A pilot, a navigator who is also the weapons control officer, and a radar/sonar/lidar operator. It is an amalgam of a surface patrol/torpedo boat, a high speed submersible utilizing cavitation/bubble technology, and a weapons platform with some amazing high tech weapons and some basic slug throwing guns and torpedoes. In a pinch it can transport up to thirty people and still fight effectively. Its power comes from a nuclear-powered HMD or hydro-magneto-drive, similar to the Sword. It can turn in a tight circle not much more than its own length and reach speeds on the surface of over 100 knots or roughly 117 miles per hour. The submerged speed is in excess of 260 knots or 300 mph. The only possible hang-up is that it takes a trained pilot who can handle supersonic fighter aircraft and who aren't easily rattled.

Mark smiled, "How soon can we get one of these, Rob?"

Rib smiled, "There are two of them less than an hour from here and they are headed our way. And, since you, The Israeli Defense Force, and Mr. Victor Chamberlain have already invested several hundred million dollars in these two ships, they are entirely yours to decide what to do with them."

Mark smiled, "I believe we can use them ourselves."

Rob asked, "Okay, but where can you get qualified pilots?"

"We've got two of the most qualified fighter pilots in the world right here on the Sword. One of them is one of your Martial Arts instructors, Su Li. The other is Michael White, who trained Su Li. How long will it take to get them qualified on these new boats?"

Rob pursed his lips. "Probably less than a week, if they are that good already. It'll all depend on their ability to adapt to a water environment rather than air."

Let's start with classroom study tomorrow morning. Interestingly enough, it's ironic that you're the ones providing employment for the two members who are the most qualified for this job. Because it's you who took away their jobs as our pilots with the autonomous aircraft. Why aren't these boats autonomous also?"

Rob grinned, "For the same reason the "Formidable" isn't autonomous. I don't think we're yet ready to let a silicon brain fire an atomic cannon or a rail gun. These boats each have both of those weapons.

Jack tipped his head to the side. "But Rob, didn't you say that the navigator handles the weapons, not the pilot?"

Rob nodded, "Yes I did, but I also mentioned that they can be handled by one person if need be. I still want a human being in charge of the weapons.

Mark nodded, "Okay then. Commander Kelly, can you berth these two fighter boats in the area of the aircraft?"

Hugh smiled, "Of course I can. Isn't it a flipping wonderful coincidence that we have precisely enough space at an inside dock that was designed to handle multiple LSTs (Landing Ship Transports) for the Marines? And that there's a quick access port for ease of entry or exit even at slow speed on the surface. I really don't suggest trying to launch or recover them while we're submerged. You might get all your other aircraft wet."

Mark surprised the XO (Executive Officer) by mentioning, "Don't worry about that. The port is sealed closed while the ship is submerged."

Hugh smiled, "Good to know."

CHAPTER FORTY-ONE

Su Li walked into the War Room that afternoon and found Jack, Mark, Commander Kelly and Mike White already there.

Jack indicated a chair for the pretty Asian woman. When she was seated, Jack smiled at her and Mike. "We want to thank you both for quietly endure the lack of piloting time for the last year. It was a big surprise to all of us when everything switched to anonymous aircraft not needing pilots. We know it's been hard to put up with the situation and like I said, we appreciate your tolerance. I'm glad to announce that your wait is at an end, sort of."

Mike smiled, "Why "sort of?"

Mark said, "It seems we need both of your impressive talents and at the same time we're going to give you both a chance to expand your resumes with a unique opportunity to diversify your experience levels."

Su Li looked a bit grumpy, "Sirs, could you please can the sales pitch and get to the point?"

Commander Kelly smiled, "Subtle as ever Si Li. I am going to have the honor of having you guys work part time for me in the Crossfire Navy. It seems that we need people who can fly fighter jets under water. Major White and you are apparently the only people qualified to pilot our latest high-tech fighter craft. The only difference is you'll need to be able to do this on the surface of the seas and under them also."

Su Li's eyebrows rose, "You want us to drive boats? I don't think so."

Jack laughed, "Not just any boats, Su Li. How about if we call them weapons platforms with firepower equal to the "Formidable" and capable of moving through the water at over three hundred miles per hour?"

Su Li sat there for a minute. "Pilot a boat that can move four hundred and forty feet per second and has a nuclear cannon and a rail gun?"

Hugh nodded, "Not only that, but multiple cannons and torpedoes and mines."

She smiled, "I could be my own pint-sized battleship. Okay. I'm interested, what do the boats look like?"

Jack used Rob's baby projector and displayed the photos of the boat and interior shots, including one of the pilot's position. The control panel was more than complex with switches, levers, multiple view screens and a four-point harness at each position.

Su Li looked at Jack, "It looks a lot like the Ghost Aircraft."

Jack made a wry face, "That makes sense since the same group designed both of them."

Su Li asked, "How about training on these boats?"

Mark nodded, "Starts tomorrow morning for both of you."

Mike spoke for the first time. "How much training will it take to make us efficient?"

Jack shrugged his shoulders. "Captain Robert Maxwell says, as ace fighter jockeys you two are already capable of high efficiency in these Warcraft, all you'll need is familiarization and a small amount of practice."

Mike looked at Su Li and some subtle communication took place between them. Mike nodded, "Can we get a manual to study today?"

Mark smiled, "Let's go down to the hanger deck and inspect the boats and see if we can't scrape up something. The Engineering Techs that brought them over should have something like that laying around."

On the way to the hanger deck Su Li tapped Mark on the arm. "What name did they give these craft?"

Mark grinned at her, *"Sealeathal Attack Ships"*. In the same generation as their *"Helleathal Drones and Missiles"* like the ones that took out the ten Russian stealth fighters near Japan."

Su Li thought for a few seconds, "I think I'll name the one I use as *"She-Lethal"* and Mike can call his *"He-Lethal"*."

Mike grunted, "If it's alright with you, I'll just call mine *"Viper One"* because it's going to be one bad sea snake!"

They walked over to the dock where the two ships were berthed and it was somewhat shocking to approach them because they were a lot larger in reality as they seemed in the photos. Su Li reached over from the dock and placed her hand on the almost eighty-foot-long ominous shape. It was like she had to touch it to commune with it. She leaned back and grinned. "Oh yeah, we're going to work well together."

Talking to the Techs produced a couple of two-inch thick manuals for each craft and a great deal of high praise for the virtues of the class of ship. The six of the team were given a quick tour outside and inside one of the ships.

After that, Jack dismissed the two pilots until the next morning.

As Su Li and Mike walked away to study their books, they talked excitedly with a great deal of hand waving.

Jack smiled, "I think they are happy again."

Mark and Hugh Kelly agreed. Hugh laughed, "Su Li had a gleam in her eyes and very soon I wouldn't want to be an enemy she had orders to hunt down and deal with."

Mark looked at Jack. "Will those craft be allowed to use the protection field like the Sword?"

Jack thought about that. "I don't see why not. God said we could use the field on any ship or aircraft we have. Because of the large number of enemies we've made and because there are literally millions of people who want to kill the thirty-five of us. It's the whole balance thing."

Mark thought about that. "Okay, but do we fix one of the Force Generators to the craft or simply pray for continual coverage?"

Jack frowned, "That's above my knowledge level." "Raquel".

Raquel appeared, "I don't know the answer to that question, either. Let me ask Hugo." He stood there for all of about five seconds when Hugo appeared. Looking like a friendly grandfather, Hugo smiled at the two men. "The difference is negligible because either one is based on the belief that God will provide the protection you seek. I would recommend you use the Force Generators on ships and aircraft because the protection stays with the vehicle and not just one person."

Hugo disappeared. Raquel looked at both men. "I feel certain you both understand this, but, for my sake I need to remind you that the protection field is not only designed to level the combat field. But it is only available when a person is doing the Most High's work. Personal or aggressor use does not qualify a person for that protection. You've certainly noticed that when using the field for destruction you have always had the Most High's permission or been commanded to do so prior to that form of use.

Mark laughed, "Raquel, I'm surprised to hear that. Haven't heard it before, but that's fine. It seems that's the only reason we've ever had it before. To do God's will and frankly. I don't remember when we have had any time to do anything else. Thanks for letting us know though."

The Archangel stared through Mark for a bit before he responded. "The Most High just reminded me that your character and that of everyone on the team was a major factor He selected each of you. Your faith keeps the enemy from controlling you and your normal way of living precludes your misuse of the power He gives you. Not all humans could resist misusing that much power. I'm again happy I know all of you. Remember, we still don't know what Satan has planned as a revenge against all of you. If you need me, I will be ready."

Raquel faded out of sight only to have the Angel Rose swirl into the room. "Jack, Mark, Go to the War Room immediately! Oh Good night, what am I saying?" She grabbed an arm on each man ant they appeared in the War Room. As she released them, Mark rubbed his arm where she had grabbed him and looked at her, "Ouch," Then he smiled at her. "Just kidding."

The rest of the Core Team ran into the room and grabbed their seats. Rose looked around. "We have determined what the enemy of all that's good has set in motion as his revenge against the Crossfire Team!"

CHAPTER FORTY-TWO

The Angel looked angry. "Satan has put in motion a diabolical plan to force all people on the planet to destroy your team or face demonic assault! All governments, all private citizens, police, military, and nuclear command forces are now dedicated to save their people.

To ensure total dedication to his will, Satan openly commanded his demons to go into the religious centers for every major religion on Earth and, on television and video, killed every man, woman, and child in the vilest and cruelest ways possible

The Most High's Warrior Angels were successful in repelling the demons in some places. But, to save themselves and their families, the majority of the Earth's inhabitants have decided that to keep Satan from slaughtering them it would be best to destroy the team!"

There was no panic or fear in the fourteen people in the War Room. They discussed various ways to prevent Satan from capitalizing on his threats. After twenty minutes, Mark stood up. "People! Listen to me. Satan is doing this because I called his bluff in China. Now, he has upped the ante again and is trying to get the population of the world to get even for him.

"I have been asking the Father what our role is in this matter. The very clear answer is that we must convince him to abandon this course and make him suffer for the unwarranted murders he ordered. So ... Let's see, so far we've hit him with two nuclear weapons and reduced his favorite place in the demonic kingdom to rubble with HARP. He apparently hasn't gotten the concept that when he strikes us, we pay him back much worse than whatever he did to us."

Mark shook his head, "Well he can't say we didn't warn him. I think it's time to play hardball with him. Are you all with me?"

The response was unanimous and loud. Laura asked, "With three major weapon strikes already, what are you going to do for an encore?"

Mark smiled, "Something so horrible he'll never expect it and it won't leave him any way to retaliate." I need to check on some things and some resources first. I'll let you know all about it tomorrow."

The next morning, Mark assembled the entire Crossfire Team in the mess hall. "You should all know about the latest attacks yesterday that Satan is using to force all people on Earth to want to destroy us to save themselves. True?"

The other team members all nodded or said "Yes".

Mark smiled, "And you all know that we have warned him repeatedly that if he continues to escalate his attacks we will respond in kind?" Again the affirmatives were complete.

"This publically aired murdering of thousands of innocents requires an ultimate response. I have arranged just such a response. The Father has released all team members to start destroying every demon in the demonic domain beginning with the operations center controlling these new attacks and move outward in all directions. No demon is to be left alive, no infrastructure is to be left intact, anywhere. This will continue until Satan surrenders and reverses his efforts to use the world to destroy us. Questions?"

David asked, "How will so few survive against his millions of demons when our defensive fields aren't allowed in that realm?"

Mark replied, "Every team member battling in the demonic realm will have a functioning defensive field preventing any force from hurting them."

Jack frowned, "The Savior agreed with Satan that we would not be allowed to use our defensive fields in the demonic realm."

Mark agreed, "That is true. We can't use our fields in that realm."

Alexis said, "I'm confused, how can we fight that many demons without the fields?"

Christi laughed, "I know why! We aren't going. Good plan, Mark."

Mark smiled, "Right, because we won't be there. Members of the eleven other teams have volunteered to go into the demonic realm to do the battle for the Lord in lieu of the thirty-five of us. They have not been restricted as far as their defensive fields go. Yahshua agreed with Satan that the Crossfire Team could not use their fields. Only the Crossfire Team, not the other teams."

Laura asked, "What was the response from the other teams? Have any of them ever been in the demonic realm before?"

Mark shook his head, "No, none of them."

Jack asked, "How many members on the other teams volunteered to do battle?"

Mark smiled again, "All of them, I guess. Roughly five hundred and twenty or so."

Christi asked, "Could some of us join other teams for the duration and use our fields?"

Mark shook his head, "That's a novel idea Christi, but the answer is no, I already asked. God said He has other tasks that we are needed for during this time. Okay folks, you are all dismissed and can return to duty but, be ready to go at a moment's notice."

After the team dispersed, Jack asked Mark, "Aren't you a little disappointed that it isn't us taking the battle to Satan this time?"

Mark slapped Jack on the back. "Only a little bit, because we won't be there, the leaders of the other teams are going to see that Satan firmly understands that this was Mark Connelly's idea. I just couldn't resist rubbing a little salt into his wounds."

CHAPTER FORTY-THREE

As the two men talked about the events going on, the strident "Team Alarm" sounded throughout their section of the Sword.

Jack turned around and called Major Reaper. "Alright Ethan, what's going on?"

The Com/Sec Leader responded immediately. The Kidon have requested an emergency scramble of the Crossfire Team to the area of downtown Tel Aviv, Israel. Over a hundred demons are attacking the Synagogue where your step-father and uncle, Christi's mother, and Sensei Grady are at presently. I'm also receiving an urgent call from the FBI, a Gary Rhodes that an unknown number of physically present demons are attempting to kidnap or kill; himself, a CBI operative and others in Denver, Colorado. There are two Pastors also asking for our help in the U.S. A Frank Mullinsin Chicago, Illinois, and a Tim Carsonin Denver, Colorado. They both say that they are being either hunted or attacked by physically present demons. Lastly, at least so far, Israel's Chief Rabbi Ben Chanan and his associates in Jerusalem, Israel are being beset by demons right now."

Jack looked at Mark, 'I think Satan thinks he's outsmarted us. With all the other teams involved in the demonic realm we don't have any help to respond to four different cities at the same time plus the fact that we're over four to seven thousand miles from any of those places. I think we need to ask the Father for help. Assemble the troops and divide us into six groups. Put yourself, me, Sarah, Laura, David, and Alexis in charge of one group each. Leave Christi here with Ethan, and Carol as a fast response team. I'm going to see how much Heavenly help we can get!"

Mark hit the all-call button on his communications pack as he ran out the door for the mess hall.

Jack dropped to his knees and beseeched Yahveh for help to rescue the beleaguered people. Before he could ask anything Raquel showed up with six other Angels. Jack started to stand up and before he was standing upright all eight of them were in the mess hall. Raquel and five of the Angels disappeared with five or six people. Suddenly standing by themselves, Christi, Ethan, and Carol looked at each other and left for the COMM/SEC Department.

Jack and five members of the SOG, along with Raquel appeared five paces away from a huge group of demons and for the six team members their armor and swords exploded into sight. Led by Jack and the Archangel, everyone waded into the demons. There were so many, individual target selection wasn't necessary. As the demons were caught unaware at first, God's warriors reigned havoc on them. More than half of the demons were killed in the first ten minutes. Jack noticed the righteous anger of the Lord was building in power with each new enemy faced.

The newly arrived rescuers continued to decimate the demons at an accelerating rate as they fought their way into the Synagogue. The demons had lost most of their forces outside and there were only ten demons inside. Nine of these demons were the sleek, human-like upper level demons and far more proficient with a sword. Which bought them very little as the attacking humans and the Archangel were protected by the shield of God's power. Three minutes later there was only one demon left.

He was a high upper level demon, probably above an Archangel in power. He couldn't hurt the team members or the Archangel due to the protective fields but their weapons weren't strong enough to hurt him either. Seeing the impasse, Jack prayed that the Father would give him the power he'd used to destroy Xndalius earlier.

As Jack felt the power build in him beyond any scale he could think of, he focused on this new demon and loudly said, **"In the name and by the authority of Yahveh God, I destroy all creatures of this type in Heaven or Hell or in the human dimension!"**

The demon shattered into so many fragments it looked like a pillar of sand as it collapsed onto the floor. Jack knelt and prayed his thanks to God and Yahshua. He added a comment to his prayer. "Father, I hope I did not overstep my authority by eliminating all demons of that type rather than a single creature. Since Satan is not creative, I believed that he would put such a creature over all of the attacking groups. In this way we would eliminate the beasts in all the operations at one time since we would be unable to defeat their level of unbelief with the weapons we have. If I was wrong Father, I confess my sin of pride and ask your forgiveness. I pray this in Your Son's name, Amen."

Jack heard the voice of Yahshua in his mind. *"Jack, what you did was what I spoke into your mind. This action I wanted you to do and you were right to believe what you did. There was no sin in it. Be at peace."*

Relieved, Jack walked into the next room and was able to hug all of his family and friends. The Sensei was glad to see Jack. "Thank Yahveh and Yahshua you were able to rescue us. If it hadn't been for God's protection, we would have all been killed an hour ago."

Jack heard Raquel's voice in his head. Then he spoke back to the Sensei, "I'm very glad we could be here to help all of you. I love you all and pray daily for you. It's good to see you but I have to go now. I'll call you all later."

Jack smiled and then just disappeared.

He found himself back in the mess hall of the Sword. He and the five SOG members filled out their after-action reports and turned in their gear. Jack thanked the three men and two women and released them from any further duty until the next day.

About an hour later Three of the other teams appeared and went through the same routine. Finally, Mark returned with the last away team. When they were done and released Jack and Mark got a chance to discuss their events. Jack told him of the elimination of the hundred demons, especially the last one.

Mark recounted their mission to aid Rabbi Ben Chanan and the other Rabbis. It had been grueling because only Rabbi Chanan had the protection field. Thirty-seven of the other staff had been killed by the time the team arrived. As their battle progressed, Mark ran into three of the high level, indestructible demons which were battling Mark and his team. All of a sudden all three of the higher level demons fragmented and were gone. Mark smiled, "I'd seen that a couple of times before, but I didn't know if God did it or you did. That wrapped it up even though the rift stayed open, no more demons came out of it and eventually it faded out."

Mark frowned, "The Angel that took us there told me that the action this time was an integral part of Satan's plan. Apparently, he was aware that I would suggest using the other teams because he had an agreement with Yahshua that we couldn't use our protection fields in his kingdom. He set that up so he could launch an all-out blitz to capture or kill all of the second tier of Crossfire Team support personnel to hurt us or force us to give into his demands. In other words, he scammed me from the beginning this time and I fell for it. Hard as it is to admit, he is smarter than I thought he could be. If the Father hadn't translated us to all those locations, we would have lost all of them."

Jack stared at Mark. "Not the ones with the fields."

Mark nodded, "Eventually they would overcome the defensive fields. The demons were massing to overcome God's righteousness with their cumulative unrighteousness and would have killed or subdued the person."

Jack blew out a deep breath, "How do you know that?"

Mark said, "The Angel told me and when I prayed, Yahshua confirmed it. We have been dodging a bullet so far."

"Do you think they could overcome the field protecting the Sword?"

Mark shook his head. "If I understand it correctly, because of the number of his believers on this ship it would require more unrighteousness than Satan could ever muster in one place. It's only an individual that could be overwhelmed that way."

Jack relaxed, "Good, I was really worried for a moment there."

Mark smiled, "One major reason they haven't been able to do it to our group is because we are very efficient at killing off demons near us so they can't amass enough cumulative unrighteousness to overwhelm us. Unless, they bring enough upper level demons that we can't defeat. That is now almost impossible thanks to the power God allowed you to use on Earth to defeat, not only the demon facing you, but every other upper level demon anywhere."

Jack repeated his rationale for doing a type of demon rather than the single demon. "I reasoned that if there was one facing me there would be one facing each of the teams. I prayed and Yahshua told me I had made the decision He wanted me to make."

Mark tipped his head to the side as he looked at Jack. "Really? It's very good that it was approved by Him."

Jack frowned, "Why? I only took out a single level of demons that we could not overcome, that's all."

Mark's eyebrows rose. "That's all? Let me explain something. You have significantly altered the entire demonic world with that one command using that power. Satan not only instantly lost over twelve million of his highest level demons, but those twelve million were his fourteen levels of his primary control over the entire hierarchy in the demonic realm! To make that understandable in our terms it's as if you had single-handedly, instantly eliminated all of the non-commissioned officers, such as Sergeants from our military. They run the military! Without them the officers would have to deal with and command each individual soldier by themselves. That's the hand you just dealt the devil. You may have eclipsed me as his number one most-hated person."

Raquel appeared. "Gentlemen, I bring you information from Heaven. As individuals and as a team you will not have to concern yourselves with dealing with Satan or the demonic realm again. The Most High has completely eliminated Satan's ability to embody his demons from now on. That process was a product from another universe and has been wiped from all minds including the mind of Satan. It is as if it never existed."

"The embodied demons already on Earth are stranded here in their bodies and cannot return to the demonic realm. They were being controlled through the high level demon they worked for and all of those no longer exist. You and the other teams will have to track them down and dispose of them as you can."

"By the time he can do anything other than simply trying to keep order and control over his domain, your time on Earth will be over and you will be in Heaven. I want to personally thank you, for a major reduction in my workload and that of all the Angels. The majority of Satan's long range plans have totally disappeared from the matrix. But, do not forget about his ability to command his human tools to give you trouble." Raquel smiled, "The use of the protective field for each person will be curtailed unless you are overwhelmed and cry out to the Most High. I will still be available as will the rest of the Heavenly Host as you do the Will of the Most High on Earth." Raquel saluted them and faded out of sight.

Mark laughed, "Didn't I say, _Significantly_?"

The Crossfire Team will return in
"Desperation Crossfire"

If this story has awakened you or moved you to seek the love of Christ and His power for your life, whether you've never accepted Jesus as your savior or you've fallen away, repeat the following prayer and begin a most wonderful journey into eternal life with Him today.

Father God in heaven, As You said in Your Holy Word, (Romans 10:9) that if we confess the Lord Jesus as our God and believe in our hearts that by His Holy Spirit Yahveh God raised Jesus from the dead, we shall be saved.

(The prayer on the next page is a sample prayer when asking Jesus into your heart as your Savior. You can also pray this in your own words.)

Salvation Prayer

Dear God in heaven, I come to you in the name of Jesus. I confess to You that I am a sinner, and I am sorry for my sins and the life that I have lived; I need your forgiveness. I believe that your only begotten Son Jesus Christ shed His precious blood on the cross at Calvary and died for my sins, and I am now willing to turn from my sin.

Right now I confess Jesus as the Lord of my life and my soul. With all my heart, I truly believe that your Holy Spirit raised Jesus from the dead. Today I accept Jesus Christ as my personal Savior and according to Your Word, right now I am saved.

I thank you Jesus, for your unlimited grace, which has saved me from my sins. I thank you Jesus that your grace that never leads to license, but rather it always leads to repentance. Therefore, Lord Jesus, transform my life so that I may bring glory and honor to you alone and not to myself.

I thank you Lord Jesus, for shedding his blood in seven different places to restore me in this life and for dying for me at Calvary and giving me eternal life.

Amen.

If you just said this prayer and you meant it with all your heart, believe that you are now saved and have been born again.

You may ask, "Now that I am saved, what do I do next?" First of all, you need to get into a spirit-filled, bible-based church that teaches the Scriptures, and you need to study God's Word.

Once you have found a church home, you will want to become water-baptized by immersion. By accepting Christ, you are baptized in the spirit, but it is through water-baptism that you publically announce your obedience to the Lord Jesus. Water baptism is a symbol of your salvation from the dead. You were dead but now you live, for Jesus Christ has redeemed you for a price! The price was His atoning death on the cross. May God Bless You as you learn to walk in His light!